UNDISCIPLINED

BOOK 1.5 IN THE BRIDAL DISCIPLINE SERIES

GOLDEN ANGEL

Printed in the United States of America

Cover art by Wicked Smart Designs
Edited by MJ Edits

Thank you so much for picking up my book!

Would you like to receive a free story from me as well? Join the Angel Legion and sign up for my newsletter!

ACKNOWLEDGMENTS

I have a lot of people to thank for helping me with this book. My Maries, my power houses! Marie for all her help with editing and the continuity issues that I occasionally struggle with (I swear, she remembers all the things that I can't). Another Marie, for her incredibly close attention to detail, especially when it comes to commas, mixed-up words and my excessive use of the word "that". Katherine, for her ever-lasting support, encouragement and suggestions. Michelle for her comments and suppositions, which sent me in a different direction several times for this story, creating a much better and more satisfying plot than I'd originally had, with much more interesting character development. Sir Nick, for providing the much-needed male perspective. As always, a big thank you to all my fans, for buying and reading my work… if you love it, please leave a review!

ACKNOWLEDGMENTS

[illegible]

AUTHOR'S NOTE

Dear Reader,

If you are looking for an entirely new book, this is not that - you want Gabrielle's Discipline. This is a novella which was written at the request of readers to see the events of Philip's Rules from Gabrielle and Felix's perspective. This is a re-tread of Philip's Rules from their points of view. I don't think it is required reading at all to enjoy Gabrielle's Discipline, but if you wanted a peek into their thoughts and a deeper understanding of their characters, this is a great way to get it.

Thank you so much for reading and I hope you enjoy!

~Angel

A LISTING OF CHARACTERS, TITLES AND RELATIONSHIPS

Philip Stanley the Marquess of Dunbury married Cordelia Astley, the Dowager-Baroness of Hastings

Lady Gabrielle Astley – stepdaughter to Cordelia Astley, now ward of the Marquess of Dunbury

Hugh Stanley, Viscount Petersham, married to Irene, cousin to Philip Stanley

Edwin Villiers, Lord Hyde, married to Eleanor (sister to Hugh)

Thomas Hood, eldest son of Viscount Hood

Walter Hood, second son of Viscount Hood

Felix Hood, youngest son of Viscount Hood

Isaac Windham, Duke of Manchester

Benedict Windham, brother to the Duke of Manchester

Arabella Windham, sister to the Duke of Manchester

Christopher Irving, Earl of Irving, married to Marjorie Irving

Wesley Spencer, Earl of Spencer, married to Cynthia

Alex Brooke, Lord Brook – heir to the Marquess of Warwick, married to Grace

CHAPTER 1

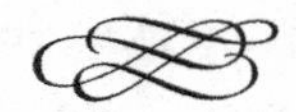

It was an auspicious and shocking day… Felix Hood's best friend was getting married today. Although Philip Stanley, the Marquess of Dunbury, was three years older than Felix, somehow Felix hadn't thought this day would come so soon. Then again, as a younger son to a Viscount, Felix didn't have the same responsibilities that Philip did. His eldest brother, Thomas, would be the one stepping into their father's shoes, and his son would follow him; unlike Philip, who had already inherited his title and thus needed his own heir.

However, Felix also happened to know that Philip wasn't just marrying to ensure his lineage; he also happened to be rather enamored of his fiancé. Felix was looking forward to meeting this paragon who had captured his friend's attention.

As he walked up to the Dunbury house, the sound of voices in the alley beside it caught his attention, as did a glimpse of a pale dress. Any kind of lightly colored finery seemed out of place in the servants' alley, which is what caused him to slow his pace, peering down the narrow walkway. A young woman, obviously a young lady, was leaning forward and talking to two little girls, obviously servants' get, going by their much simpler attire. Her skirts melded to her backside, which was nicely rounded, and immediately drew his attention – as it would any experienced rake. Especially one with his proclivities.

Both little girls were clutching their dolls and very gingerly holding what looked to be two dresses in miniature, made with cloth much finer than that of their own clothing. The dolls' dresses were something he would expect to see a child of noble birth clothing their dolls with, not servants' children. His eyebrows rose at the sight.

"We be eva' so careful, miss," one of the little girls assured the young lady earnestly. "We promise."

"I'm glad you like them," said the young lady, with a little laugh, her tones much more cultured than the little imps she was talking to. Although Felix couldn't see her face, he admired her light brown hair, which glinted with red and gold highlights wherever the sun caught it, and the well-proportioned figure of her backside. The two girls were staring up at her as if she was a goddess, as well they might. He doubted their dolls had ever received such finery before. "Now run along, I have to go."

That last was said with a bitterly resigned sigh, as if she would have much preferred to stay in the alley with the two little girls. They thanked her again and then ran off down the alley, obviously ecstatic over their good fortune, while the young lady slipped back into the house using the servants' door. Felix's eyebrows felt like they'd taken up a permanent position on his forehead as he wondered if he'd just received his first glimpse of Philip's new bride.

If so, he certainly approved… although if her front was as attractive as her backside, he was also going to be eaten up with envy at his friend's good fortune. Generous, thoughtful, *and* endowed with posterior charms? She seemed like the perfect woman. Perhaps he'd be in luck and she was one of the guests… preferably a widow or married with an inattentive husband and a desire to have her passions awakened.

~

"I NOW PRONOUNCE YOU, man and wife."

A sense of utter hopelessness rose in Gabrielle at the words. Her stepmother was now married to a man that Gabrielle barely knew, but was now responsible for her. A cold man, who looked at Gabrielle in a distant, almost disdainful manner that reminded her harshly of her own father before he'd passed. Her fingers clutched the bouquet she was holding tighter as she kept her smile pasted onto her face. The simple joy she'd received from gifting the housekeeper's daughters with dolls' clothes had worn off fairly quickly once she'd been recalled to her real life.

Gabrielle liked children much more than she liked adults, especially adults of the nobility. The servants in her life had always been kinder to her than even her own family, and children were so easily pleased with whatever small tokens she could give them. She found the working class easier to talk to than any of her peers. They couldn't be friends, of course; none of them were comfortable crossing that line and actually befriending her, but they were often kind. Dunbury's servants seemed to have a mixed opinion of her, but that was likely due to the Marquess' influence.

She hadn't liked the Marquess of Dunbury when she'd met him and, truthfully, she liked him even less now. Not only had he been dismissive of Gabrielle from the start, but since meeting him, Cordelia had barely had a moment for Gabrielle. Yes, there were times when Gabrielle couldn't stand Cordelia, but she hadn't wanted to give up her stepmother's attention either. Logically, she knew it hadn't been Cordelia's fault that Gabrielle's father had no love for his daughter. He hadn't before he'd married Cordelia either.

But Cordelia was young and beautiful, and she'd become the Baron's main focus once they were wed – or at least, getting an heir on her had become his main focus. Then he'd died, and Gabrielle had had Cordelia all to herself. For the first time in her life, since her own mother had died, she'd been the center of someone's attention. Cordelia had cossetted her, comforted her, and been devoted to helping Gabrielle through her mourning... of course, once they'd come out of mourning, Cordelia had set about finding a second husband. Bitterly jealous that she'd lost Cordelia's attention so quickly, Gabrielle had chased off several of Cordelia's suitors when they'd come calling. Often by flirting with them, figuring it served Cordelia right. Why should she get a second husband when Gabrielle hadn't even had her first? What made Cordelia so special that all these men wanted to court her?

She didn't question Cordelia's change in attitude towards Gabrielle; she'd never expected to hold Cordelia's attention anyway. No one ever truly wanted Gabrielle.

Still, it seemed to have worked at first and Gabrielle had started to hope that perhaps she might even be able to successfully poach one of Cordelia's suitors and have her own husband... or that Cordelia would give up and then refocus her attentions back on her step-daughter. Instead, Gabrielle had been left at home with a hired companion while Cordelia had gone away to a house party on her own and come back engaged. In a last ditch effort at keeping her little world intact, Gabrielle had made a play for the Marquess, hoping to send him packing too, but instead all she'd done was rouse disgust in him. Just not enough for him to forgo marrying Cordelia.

The Marquess didn't care for Gabrielle, but that didn't stop Cordelia from marrying him. It felt like the worst sort of betrayal by her stepmother, who claimed that she was looking out for Gabrielle's best interests by marrying a man who obviously disdained her.

She told herself she didn't care. She told herself she hated Cordelia anyway, she didn't need her stepmother's attention. And she certainly hated her new guardian.

The only joys she'd had in the past months had been stolen moments of playing with the servants' children and doing whatever she could to make Cordelia's life harder. It was petty, but it was all Gabrielle had. Why should Cordelia get everything? It wasn't fair. But then, life was never fair, especially Gabrielle's life.

Following the Marquess and Marchesse down the aisle, Gabrielle didn't even glance at the man escorting her. She was too busy trying to keep from bursting into tears, wondering what was going to become of her now that Cordelia was married to such a cold man.

~

FELIX WAS NOT USED to being ignored. Especially not by a member of the fairer sex. In fact, he couldn't remember the last time it had happened. Before the wedding, Philip had asked him to keep an eye on Miss Gabrielle Astley, Philip's bride's stepdaughter. The daughter of a Baron, once she'd had her come-out she'd be known as Lady Gabrielle, but she was currently a mere miss. Apparently she had a shrewish disposition. Philip had described her as attractive, but he truly hadn't done her justice.

Neither had Felix's own thoughts, because he immediately recognized her as the young woman he'd seen in the alley.

Resplendent in her cream and green dress, which matched the lovely bride's, Miss Astley was just as attractive from the front as she had been from the back, despite the pout on her lips. Unlike the bride's dark tresses, her masses of light brown hair were piled on top of her head and decorated with pearl combs, setting off her creamy complexion, and thickly-lashed green eyes. Slim figured, she was still blessed with delightful feminine curves, even if they weren't overly abundant. There were two high spots of color on her cheeks, and her eyes were shiny and bright, and entirely focused on Cordelia and Philip. There was a hint of malice in them, but also a sadness.

Philip had mentioned that Gabrielle had flirted with him, even after knowing that he was engaged to Cordelia. Could it be that she truly was attracted to her new stepfather and was envious of Cordelia's marriage? But no, that didn't quite fit with the way she was looking at them. She seemed almost… forlorn. But by the time they'd exited the church, that hint of vulnerability was gone, buried under haughtiness. She was an entirely different person than he'd seen in the alley and the contrast intrigued him.

Before the receiving line, Philip had introduced them so that he could properly carry on a conversation with Miss Astley, but she'd barely given him a second glance.

Between well-wishers, Felix leaned down to whisper in her ear. "Congratulations on your new family, Miss Astley. As Philip's best friend, I'm sure we'll be seeing quite a bit of each other."

The smile that he received in return looked forced, her lovey green eyes were dull despite the curving of her lips. There was no energy or sincerity in her voice when she responded. "I look forward to it."

He frowned, unused to having to exert himself to engage in conversation with a lady. Usually they were tripping over themselves to speak with him. They both smiled and greeted the next guest, before they had a moment to breathe again. Taking her silence as a challenge, Felix decided to try again. He was still curious about why she'd given dolls' clothes to the servants' children, but there wasn't really a polite way to ask, so he was forced to take a different conversational route.

"I'm sorry I was unable to make your acquaintance before this, I was traveling through Scotland, taking care of some business for my brother."

"I've always wanted to travel," she returned a bit wistfully, her focus turning inward, which wasn't exactly the effect he'd been trying to receive. "Is Scotland very nice this time of year?"

"Depends on which part you visit," he said, giving her his best, most charming smile, inviting her to join in it with him. "I was on the coast and it was quite temperate, but further North, the Highlands are always cold no matter the time of year."

Another guest stepped up to them, the widowed Dowager Countess of Hazelmore, with whom Felix had had a dalliance the year before. He kept his face smooth as she simpered up at him; more than once she'd made it clear that he'd be welcome back into her bed. Her gown today was rather scandalous for a wedding, low-cut enough to show off an ample view of her charms, and the way she was leaning forward nearly allowed him to look straight down into her dress.

"How lovely to see you again, Felix," she said, her voice breathy and hinting at intimacies; entirely inappropriate for their current locale and the fact that Miss Astley was well within hearing. "London has been quite dull while you were away."

"You are looking quite fetching, as always, my lady," he responded, standing stiffly and not quite catching her eye, ignoring her statement. The bloody woman didn't need any encouragement. "Thank you for your attendance, I'm sure the Marquess and Marchesse appreciate your presence."

Either oblivious to or unwilling to acknowledge his subtle rebuff, she put her hand on his arm, completely ignoring Miss Astley, who was fidgeting beside him. "Perhaps you and I could… catch up during the meal."

"My regrets, my lady, but the Marquess has requested I escort Miss Astley here; the Marchesse's stepdaughter and his new ward, you know." He gave the brazen woman a patently false smile as he shook her off of his arm.

Beside him, Miss Astley had gone stiff as a board, and he couldn't blame her. It was unconscionable that the Dowager Countess had tried to proposition him in front of an innocent young miss. He doubted the exchange had done him any favors in her esteem.

"Oh, how dutiful of you," Lady Hazelmore said, her gaze turning to Miss Astley. She swept her eyes over the younger woman and then turned back to him, patently dismissing her. Anger brimmed in him, and he wished that he didn't have to play the gentleman, because Lady Hazelmore certainly deserved a set down. "I had heard the new Marchesse and Miss Astley are just come in from the country; it's so kind of you to spend your time assisting the Marquess in acclimating them."

Blessedly, Philip's cousin, Viscount Petersham, and his wife had finished congratulating Philp and his bride, and Lady Hazelmore ceded her position to them, otherwise Felix didn't know if he would have been able to remain polite in the face of her thinly veiled disdain for the Astleys. He glanced at Miss Astley, who was no longer even pretending to smile as she nodded in response to the Petershams' pleasantries.

Once they had stepped away, Felix cleared his throat, feeling the need to reassure the young woman.

"Pay no attention to Lady Hazelmore and her ilk," he said in a low voice. "Her opinion is worthless."

Miss Astley didn't even look up at him, instead her gaze was fixed upon a point in the distance. His heart ached for her. With all her time in the country, he very much doubted that she was used to the backbiting, viperous ways of the *ton.*

"Your stepmother is a lovely woman, you must feel very blessed to have her." He paused, waiting for some kind of response, but none was forthcoming. "The Marquess will take good care of you both."

"I'm sure he'll take very good care of his wife," Miss Astley responded, loudly enough to be heard by the people around him. The expression on her face was completely blank, as if the young woman he'd just been speaking with had disappeared entirely, to be completely covered by this hostile facade. "After all, he does need his heir."

Astounded, Felix bit his tongue. This wasn't at all the young woman he'd observed beforehand… what had just happened? Frowning, he did his best to dispel the assumptions Miss Astley was obviously making about her stepmother's marriage.

BEING SEATED NEXT to the most handsome man she'd ever met was doing absolutely nothing for Gabrielle's temperament. It was like today had been thought up by the Devil as a special kind of hell for her to endure. Not only was Cordelia being married to her second husband, when Gabrielle had never even had a suitor, but the man dancing attendance on Gabrielle was already quite taken with Cordelia and obviously already disliked Gabrielle. They'd almost started to have a nice conversation and then that… woman had reminded Gabrielle how unsophisticated and ignorant she was, especially compared to the women Mr. Hood was probably used to spending time with. When he'd made it clear that he was watching over her as a favor to the happy couple… well she'd entirely lost control of her temper.

For just a few minutes, she'd thought he was truly interested in speaking with her, and it had been so… lovely. She cursed herself for being fool enough to think that someone as handsome as him, as sophisticated as him, might actually be interested in her for any reason other than it was his duty.

After she'd lost control of her tongue, he kept complimenting her stepmother, as if she didn't already know Cordelia's virtues by heart. She'd heard plenty about them from her father as he went over all the reasons he'd married Cordelia and how it would benefit his heir - once Cordelia bore him. But Cordelia had failed, there was no heir... not that it had stopped her father from focusing all his attention on Cordelia in hopes that the happy event might still occur. Right up until the moment of his death - he'd called Cordelia into the room to ask if she might be with child. He'd never called for Gabrielle, and he'd passed from the world without seeing her for one last time.

Despite failing to give her first husband his heir, Cordelia was still having her second, perfect wedding, with her cold, perfectly handsome husband, while the man's perfect best friend, Mr. Felix Hood, was watching over Gabrielle for them. Ensuring she did nothing to upset their special day, hovering over her like a specter, and scowling every time she said something negative about Cordelia. He was incredibly handsome, with thick black hair and black eyes that made him look dangerous and exciting, broad shoulders and a trim waist, and his legs filled out his breeches quite nicely. More than one lady had come to flirt with him, yet he hadn't left Gabrielle's side and had exchanged more than once glance with the Marquess.

The first time in her life that she had a man dancing attendance on her, and it was all so precious Cordelia wouldn't have to pay any attention to her.

Gabrielle was so bitter, she wished she could spit on the floor to rid her mouth of the taste.

Even though she was new to society, she knew she should have made her come-out at least a year ago, if not two. She was nineteen, which put her at a disadvantage to the younger, fresher ladies. Perhaps if Cordelia had taken her to the Irvings' house party, Gabrielle could have landed a husband as well. Instead, she was completely displaced… unwelcome in her old home (the new Baron was as uninterested in her presence as her father had been) and now an obvious burden in her new one. What newly wedding couple wanted a debutante ward to wrangle with? She was sure she'd be leg-shackled to the first blighter that asked.

If she was lucky, perhaps he wouldn't be too horrid.

She couldn't help but glance at Mr. Hood, who was conversing charmingly with everyone. He was very handsome. And kind. If he wasn't constantly endorsing Cordelia, he'd be a pleasant companion… and if they weren't talking about her stepmother, Gabrielle was sure she could be too. Although, he didn't seem to be interested in talking to her about anything but her stepmother.

"Dunbury is such a lovely estate," said a lady sitting across from Mr. Hood, smiling encouragingly at Gabrielle and interrupting her ruminations. "Have you been to see it yet?"

Something wicked stirred inside Gabrielle. She was so tired of being reminded that her home was no longer her home, and that she hadn't even stepped foot in her supposed "new" home. While Dunbury House in London was where they were staying for the Season, Dunbury estate was where they'd be in residence the remainder of the year. Or once the Marquess had tired of his new bride, the way the Baron had.

"No, I'm sure I'll have plenty of time to admire it when Cordelia is with child," Gabrielle said in a bored tone. "After all, that's where we'll be shuttled off once the Marquess has done his duty."

The woman gasped quietly and several of the other diners looked at Gabrielle askance, but she didn't care anymore. Why should she? Cordelia shouldn't expect anything less from her new husband, and Gabrielle wasn't going to pretend. Nor was she going to hope that the Marquess would be any different from her father.

Fingers grasped her arm in a gentle but unyielding grip as Mr. Hood leaned in, his breath hot on her ear. A strange shimmer of excitement went through her body at his nearness... and then he ruined it.

"Not one more word out of you. I'm warning you now. If you can't keep your mouth shut or be polite, you will find yourself over my knee before the sun goes down and we'll see if I can't spank the nastiness out of you. Philip told me to keep you in line, and I will not fail him in that."

Any retort she might have made choked in her throat, as indignation, fear, and the urge to cry all collided inside her chest.

He'd seemed so nice and now… The Marquess had told Mr. Hood that he could beat her? For a few words? Even Gabrielle's father hadn't tried to completely silence her; she'd always been allowed the verbal outlet to vent her frustrations and unhappiness. But she didn't want to be beaten either. The one time her father had slapped her across her face, it had split her lip and made her cheek swell, making it hard for her to eat for days.

She felt her chest tighten as she turned her head away from him, hiding her pain and the evidence of more betrayal by Cordelia behind her social smile. The smile that she'd perfected as a young girl. It was a familiar mask, a safe mask, and the only expression that would be deemed acceptable.

Scraping up her backbone, Gabrielle sat up straight and determinedly ignored the man sitting next to her. The rest of the meal, she didn't say one more word to him, but she bent herself to being as sweet as she could to everyone else. She could feel him watching her out of the corner of his eye as she laughed and chattered. It was utterly exhausting to keep up the act, but she wouldn't give him an excuse to raise his hand to her. Even more infuriating was when he seemed pleased with her performance, and she actually felt relieved whenever she sensed his approval.

By the time the meal was over, she was completely wrung out. She tried to head to Cordelia, seeing her stepmother as the only haven of safety amongst this crowd of strangers, but the Marquess' cousin

Lady Hyde was suddenly there, taking her arm and tugging her in another direction.

"Come with me, Gabrielle," Lady Hyde said, her voice surprisingly gentle. She'd been rather harsh with Gabrielle earlier, while Cordelia had been dressing for the wedding, probably because Gabrielle hadn't been able to stop herself from needling her stepmother with some rather cruel observations, but at least she didn't seem to look down on Gabrielle for being new to London. "I'd like to introduce you to some of my friends."

Off to the side, Mr. Hood was watching, a warning on his face. Gabrielle turned away from him with a shiver. She was sure that Cordelia wouldn't allow Mr. Hood to beat her, no matter how the Marquess felt, but Cordelia was unavailable to her right now, which meant all she could do was toe the line until she could speak with her stepmother. All the while, she could feel Mr. Hood's gaze on her, just waiting to implement his threat.

Sitting at the breakfast table, Gabrielle trembled. She'd had an hour for her rage and hurt to build... anger was so much better than fear or loneliness.

Gabrielle had stewed all night, and all morning, fear and anger chasing each other around her head like two hounds, playing tug-of-war with her emotions. So when Cordelia came in, her face wreathed in smiles, it was no wonder that Gabrielle could barely breathe for the emotion choking her.

"Good morning," Cordelia said, almost cautiously, which would have made Gabrielle happy if she wasn't already so worked up.

"Perhaps for you," Gabrielle said, glaring at her angrily. Tears sparked in her eyes, but she didn't wipe them away; she wanted to ensure Cordelia could see how upset she was. "How could you marry a man like that?"

"A man like what?" The confusion on Cordelia's face gave way to sudden wariness, and Gabrielle realized that her stepmother didn't know. Some of the betrayal that she was feeling subsided and the words came tumbling out of her mouth as tears spilled over her cheeks. Part of her wanted to shock Cordelia, to tear away some of the happiness that she was obviously buoyed up by, to drag her down to the mire of misery and despair that Gabrielle was swamped with.

"His friend threatened to *hit me* last night at dinner, and he said that he had Philip's permission to do it!" Gabrielle clenched her fork tightly, drawing in a deep breath as she tried to hold back the sobs that threatened to take away her voice. Anger seemed to have vanished, giving way to fear and resentment. "I've been sitting here, waiting for you all morning, and he came in here and had breakfast, and I've been too terrified to move ever since in case he should catch me alone."

Hunching slightly, Gabrielle's eyes went to the footmen standing at the doors, whose faces were kept carefully blank as they stared straight ahead. They had been her only comfort while she'd waited... surely no one would beat her in front of the help... even if he was a lord, he wouldn't want them seeing that.

"There must be some mistake, dear," Cordelia said soothingly, moving to Gabrielle's side of the table. For once, Gabrielle couldn't help herself... she saw Cordelia's open, welcoming arms, and she lurched into them, wrapping her own arms around Cordelia's waist in a desperate plea for protection. The only thing familiar to her in this entire house was Cordelia and she clung to her as if the woman was her only port in a storm. Cordelia stroked her hair, although she had to be shocked at Gabrielle's action. Gabrielle couldn't remember ever hugging Cordelia. "I would never allow anyone to hit you and I don't think Philip would either. This must just be some kind of misunderstanding..."

The sensation of betrayal hit hard again and Gabrielle pulled away immediately, now that she knew the comfort she sought wasn't to be found there. "I should have known you wouldn't believe me. You don't care what happens to me at all now that you're married to someone else. No one ever cares what happens to me."

Burying her face in her hands, Gabrielle sobbed piteously.

Cordelia wrapped her up in her arms from behind, holding her even if Gabrielle no longer welcomed her touch.

"I do care, I do, Gabby," she said, bravely taking the nickname that Gabrielle had never allowed her to use. Gabrielle grasped Cordelia's hand, squeezing it... for once she didn't mind Cordelia using her nickname. Only her father had ever called her Gabby and only when he was in one of his rare moods where he wanted to indulge her. "I will speak to Philip. You have no need to be frightened. I'll go speak with him right now."

"Thank you," Gabrielle whispered, turning her head to burrow it into Cordelia's shoulder.

"You should go to your room and compose yourself," Cordelia said softly, patting Gabrielle's back. She looked up at one of the footmen, who immediately met her gaze. "Please escort my stepdaughter to her room, and do not let anyone delay her."

"Yes, my lady," the footman said immediately, coming forward.

Sniffling, Gabrielle stood, extricating herself from Cordelia's arms. She still felt as though she was trembling all over. While she knew that she had probably sounded hysterical... well she still felt that way. Yesterday had been too much for her even before Mr. Hood had threatened her.

She would go to her room and work on embroidering the doll's dress she'd bought for the daughter of one of the maids. That would keep her hands busy and give her something nice to distract herself with.

THE HUNTING HOUND nosed through two of her pups, who were growling over a piece of rag, both wanting to play with it. Felix couldn't help but grin, watching the two balls of fur. They were cute and fluffy now, but their dam was one of the best Philip had ever had and Felix had been trying to buy one of her pups for years. Philip had always teased him by saying he'd give Felix one as a wedding present, and Felix would groan and threaten to steal one of them instead.

Heavy footsteps warned him of Philip's approach, as the other man came to join him, leaning on the fence.

"All six still here I see."

"For now." A smile quirked Felix's lips as he gave Philip a sidelong look. Philip grinned at first, and then sobered. Seeing the change of expression, Felix's became more serious as well.

"What happened with Miss Astley last night?" Philip asked.

"One too many cutting little remarks," Felix said, frowning. He shook his head, his dark eyes serious, making him look almost brooding. "She's too green to realize that her insinuations will reflect badly on her first, and then on you and Cordelia - although not for the reasons she thinks." By which he meant that the *ton* would censure Cordelia for not instructing her stepdaughter on how to behave and Philip for his lack of control over her. It was doubtful that anyone would believe her slurs, but they would negatively affect the entire family anyway. "Eventually I told the chit that if she couldn't keep her mouth shut, she'd find herself over my knee and I'd spank that nastiness out of her." He sighed, giving Philip a rueful smile. "I realize that it wasn't appropriate, but she refused to be deflected and it was becoming quite... trying. And it worked. Once she started to behave herself, her company was much more enjoyable."

It had actually weighed on his mind all evening after he'd done it, despite the improvement in her behavior. He'd overstepped his bounds entirely and he had no business making a threat that he couldn't keep. In his defense, he'd a hard time thinking about anything else – the little brat was in need of a good spanking, and it didn't help that he couldn't stop thinking about that perfectly rounded backside that he'd initially seen. In fact, that image lingering in his mind had been what sparked his threat in the first place; he hadn't been able to stop thinking about it. Not just because he enjoyed spanking a woman's backside, but because he wanted to swat the bad behavior out of her and return her to the sweet, giving woman he'd accidentally stumbled upon beforehand. The contrast between her behaviors was as startling as it was fascinating.

"I can sympathize," Philip murmured. They both watched the

hounds play for a moment; the two pups were now tugging on the opposite ends of a knotted rag, tumbling into each other in their enthusiasm. Their dam seemed to have given up on separating them. "I hope you understand that I could never allow you to carry out such a threat as long as Gabrielle resides in *my* household." The significant look he gave Felix made him snort.

"I've no need of her dowry," Felix said immediately. He certainly hadn't come to Philip's wedding with thoughts of perpetuating his own. No matter how beautiful or complexly interesting the young woman in question was. His eyes drifted down to the hounds. "Although, she's beautiful enough. I could be convinced to take her off your hands for say... these two pups right here." He was half serious... Just because he hadn't intended to begin thinking of his own marriage didn't mean he couldn't. After all, what better way to draw his and Philip's relationship even closer? Having the beautiful Miss Astley to keep him warm at night would certainly be no hardship, and it would give him the right to govern her behavior. Preferably with a stern hand to her upturned bottom.

"Really?" drawled Philip, leaning more heavily on the fence as he studied his friend.

"You must admit, two pups and the right to spank her as I please... it wouldn't be such a bad deal."

"Even if I tell you that she's accused you of threatening to hit her to keep her in line?"

"The hell she did!" Indignant, Felix straightened, his dark eyes blazing with anger. "That little... I specifically said I would spank her, I swear. You know I would never hit a woman."

"I suspected as much," Philip said. "I made sure Cordelia knew as well."

The fury drained from Felix's face, turning to concern. Philip was his best friend, after all; if his wife were to take a dislike of Felix... well, he didn't think it would end their friendship but it would certainly strain it. "She didn't believe such a thing, did she?"

"I assured her that Gabrielle must be mistaken and that, of course, I would be the one to handle any discipline Gabrielle requires.

However, if you could exert yourself to charm Cordelia, to reassure her further, I would appreciate it. I would hate for my new wife to think I could associate with a brute."

Felix nodded. Guilt struck him hard. Had Gabrielle truly thought that he would beat her? There was a definite difference between a spanking and a beating… did she know that? He hadn't meant to make her afraid; although, now that he thought about it, she hadn't seemed fearful at the breakfast. In fact, after he'd made the threat, she'd been the very picture of charm and grace. Granted, he'd needed to give her a warning look a time or two after that, but he'd admired the way she'd deported herself for the most part. Confusion swirled in him. Had all of that been an act? Or was her accusation to Cordelia the act?

~

LEFT TO STEW AGAIN, Gabrielle felt like she was going mad. She was terrified that the Marquess would come instead of Cordelia… maybe that he would even beat her. Would he beat Cordelia too? She stared in her mirror at the haggard figure, hating the way she looked affright, but she'd had no patience for her hair this morning and didn't feel any for it now.

When the knock on her door finally came, she almost fell apart. Thankfully, it was just Cordelia at the door.

"Is he gone?" Gabrielle asked, although her tone made it sound more like a demand.

Cordelia glanced down the hall. "May I come in?" she asked, instead of answering the question.

Stepping back, Gabrielle's eyes narrowed. She pursed her lips as she shut the door behind her stepmother. Cordelia no longer looked distressed or even upset on Gabrielle's behalf. What had her new husband said to her that made anything about the situation palatable?

"Gabrielle, did Mr. Hood say that he would *hit* you or that he would *spank* you?" Cordelia asked, before Gabrielle could demand an answer to her previous question.

"It's the same thing," Gabrielle said sharply. "The man threatened to beat me, and you're quibbling about what word he used?" Her hands went to her hips as she glared at Cordelia, making Cordelia shrink into herself a bit. As if a spanking was somehow different – they both involved being hit! In fact, a spanking sounded almost worse. Naughty children were spanked, and Gabrielle was no longer a child.

"It makes a difference," Cordelia said softly.

"Either is unacceptable! I am a young lady, I refuse to be treated as a child." Fuming, Gabrielle started pacing. She sneered at Cordelia. "Apparently, your new husband isn't as enamored as you were told, if he refused to take your side already."

"It isn't my side, nor is it your side," Cordelia replied, so calmly that Gabrielle felt like slapping her. Beating, spanking… what did it matter? But Cordelia was implacable. "The Marquess reassured me that he would absolutely not allow Mr. Hood to... to discipline you. Mr. Hood overstepped his bounds, and Philip will speak with him. However-"

"Ha!" Gabrielle crowed, triumphantly. At least Mr. Hood was going to get his. Threaten to spank her would he! "That over-bearing - "

"Gabrielle," Cordelia said sharply, cutting off whatever insult Gabrielle had been about to utter. "You should also know that Philip has said he will take care of any necessary discipline in the household."

Gabrielle's jaw dropped in shock.

"You would let him beat me?" Gabrielle asked, more tears sparking in her eyes. These weren't quite real, because she knew that Cordelia would never stand for that. Once she'd become Gabrielle's stepmother, the Baron had never raised his hand to Gabrielle. Even he had realized such a step would be too far for his young wife.

"Philip would never *hit* you," Cordelia avowed, confident in that. "But-"

"Only children are spanked! I am not a child!" Contrary to her words, Gabrielle stomped her foot as she produced more tears, which she let fall down her cheeks unchecked.

"Gabby-"

"Don't call me that!" Whirling around, Gabrielle flung open the door to her bedroom. The tears had stopped as abruptly as they'd started, but the bright color in her cheeks attested that her temper had been set off. "Get out of my room!"

Cordelia left, but it didn't make Gabrielle feel any better. Spanked! Like a child!

And Cordelia would let him?

It was official… she'd finally turned her stepmother against her. Burying her face in her pillow, Gabrielle let her tears flow again.

Jermyn Street

Throwing his book against the wall, Felix wished that it made him feel better.

He was a mire of frustration, anger, and guilt. It was the last that sat most uneasily with him. Felix wasn't used to feeling guilty. Especially over a woman.

He hadn't been able to stop thinking about Miss Astley and wondering if he'd truly upset her.

He shouldn't have threatened to spank her. No matter how much damage she'd been doing to herself by letting her tongue flap freely. But how to apologize? Even more to the point, how to apologize without backing down? Whether or not his threat was appropriate, her behavior certainly hadn't been.

Miss Astley had a bit of a temper, that was certain. Obviously, she could control it when it suited her. He didn't truly mind that she had a temper either, since he'd rather liked the way her green eyes had sparked and flared. Much better than when they'd been dull and sad, the way she'd looked after the wedding ceremony.

It didn't help that he *wanted* to spank her. He wanted to take her in hand and spank the shrew right out of her; he'd seen flashes of her kinder, sweeter nature. All that charm couldn't have entirely been an act after all. And he'd noted that she treated the servants with the same kind of sweetness and charm that many of his peers wouldn't have bothered with, which spoke well of her. He didn't understand why she didn't do the same with Cordelia. It was just one of the many inconsistencies in Gabrielle's behavior that fascinated him.

CHAPTER 2

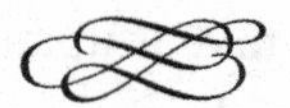

After several days of spending as little time with the Marquess as possible, Gabrielle was pleased when Cordelia took her out shopping. Shopping had been the one way in which the Baron had always indulged his daughter; as if by allowing her to buy whatever trinkets she wanted, he fulfilled his fatherly duties towards her. In her opinion, it was a poor recompense, but she had been willing to take what she could get.

Considering how miserable she'd been the past few days, she felt she deserved some fripperies. Certainly, she should get whatever she needed to help catch some gentleman's eye so she could be married off. The Marquess had made it clear that she was to have her Season and her come-out and that he expected her to receive an offer by the end of it. She didn't want to think about what would happen if she didn't receive an offer. While she doubted Cordelia would allow him to throw her out on the street, she didn't think he'd want to fund another Season for her either.

When they finally arrived home, Gabrielle was exhausted, but satisfied. She'd gotten everything she wanted to put herself forward at her best. Even better, she'd kept Cordelia from getting everything she wanted. It was the first time in ages that Gabrielle had turned the tables. For some reason, Cordelia seemed to want to placate Gabrielle and she'd taken full advantage of it. She deserved it, she figured, after having been ignored, threatened, and bullied by everyone. Perhaps Cordelia was feeling guilty for asserting that she would allow the Marquess to beat Gabrielle – good. She should.

The trouble started when Cordelia noticed a package that she hadn't seen Gabrielle purchase and demanded that she take it back.

"What? I will not! Henry, take it upstairs," Gabrielle ordered imperiously. Cordelia had never said no to her before!

"No, no, Gabrielle you knew we were at our limit, what else could you have possibly needed?" Cordelia's big brown eyes were pleading and resigned, sparking just a tinge of guilt in Gabrielle's conscience… but Cordelia was already married. She already had the perfect husband, who doted outrageously on her in a way the Baron never had. Why should she get all the happiness?

"Some lace caught my eye while I was waiting for you," Gabrielle said coolly, noting that the staff were all watching, and that Henry still hadn't followed her command. He looked frozen and torn; he was a very nice footman and had been quite kind to Gabrielle, but he obviously didn't know what to do when what she wanted clashed with what his employer's wife wanted. "And two beaded reticules that will go perfectly with the lilac gown and the pink gown that we purchased from Madame Liriene's. If you're so concerned, *you* take something back."

"We already bought you a cream reticule that will go nicely with both of those dresses," Cordelia argued. Neither she nor Gabrielle noticed that Bonnie, the maid that had accompanied them on their trip, had slipped away.

"I wanted matching ones," Gabrielle said, sniffing haughtily. "I daresay *you* would be perfectly satisfied with just the cream." Cordelia had always made do before, after all. This was the one area of Gabrielle's life where she'd ever had any control, where she'd ever gotten what she wanted – she wasn't giving that up now! She'd already given up her father, her home, and her pride, enough was enough!

"Henry, put the package by the door for now," Cordelia said, her face as stern as she could make it. It did not intimidate, but Henry moved to follow her bidding. Gabrielle gritted her teeth. She didn't blame him of course. "Gabrielle, I need to speak with you in the parlor, please."

Rolling her eyes, Gabrielle flounced down the step she was standing on. "If you insist."

"Actually, Gabrielle, I would like you to go up to your room until I send a maid for you." The staff all relaxed as the Marquess appeared in entrance to the hallway, Bonnie just a step behind him. Gabrielle scowled as soon as she saw the maid; Bonnie was one of the servants who was completely on Cordelia's side and Gabrielle knew it. "Cordelia, sweetheart, if you would come with me, I'd like to speak with you."

Gabrielle opened her mouth to protest, but one hard look from the Marquess and she turned and walked up the stairs. Stomped up the stairs, really, as much as she could in her frothy skirts. She hadn't liked the look in the Marquess' eye one bit. She already knew he was going to take Cordelia's side.

God she hated it here. She'd take the first offer of marriage she got, just to get away from this awful house.

WHEN MOLLY CAME to fetch Gabrielle, she was grateful that it was Molly and not Bonnie. Other than the housekeeper, who was constantly mothering Gabrielle as much as she could, Molly was the closest thing to a friend that Gabrielle had in the Dunbury household. She often served as Gabrielle's lady's maid and she and her husband had two darling daughters that Gabrielle enjoyed spending time with whenever she could sneak away to the servants' quarters. As far as she knew, no one had whispered a word about her activities to the Marquess or Cordelia and that was how Gabrielle preferred it. Her father had forbidden her to interact with those "lower" than them, but she wouldn't have had anyone to talk to back at home if she hadn't.

Considering the Marquess' social status and his general perception of his consequence, she doubted he'd be any different.

Molly's silent support did much to reassure Gabrielle, so when they arrived at the Marquess' study, she sailed in with her chin held high. She faltered only for a moment when she saw Cordelia seated behind the Marquess' large desk, with him standing forbiddingly at her side.

"Thank you, Molly," the Marquess said to the maid who had escorted Gabrielle from her room to the study. "Please wait out in the hall for Miss Astley. I'll call you back in when she's ready to return to her room."

Bobbing a curtsy, Molly took herself back outside, closing the door behind her. The very air in the room seemed to change, a strange tension filling it, as if everything was about to change. If Gabrielle could have lifted her chin further, she would have.

"Sit down, Gabrielle," the Marquess said, nodding to the chairs in front of the desk.

Keeping her chin high, Gabrielle came forward in a stately manner, clutching her skirts because she couldn't help herself.

"What do you have to say for yourself, about your behavior today?" he asked.

Recognizing she was being given a chance to defend herself, Gabrielle straightened even more in her seat, folding her hands in her lap over her cerulean skirt. Her eyes widened, making her look extremely innocent and a little bit younger, a tactic that had often served her well with her father, as she tilted her head to the side.

"I know I shouldn't have spoken to Cordelia so, in front of the servants," Gabrielle said, her tone falsely apologetic. She'd already thought out what she would say. "I was just so upset by her public accusations... I didn't mean to go behind her back at Fotherby's, I thought she realized that I had added to our purchases. If I'd known she wasn't paying proper attention to me, of course I would have informed her straightaway."

"You're saying Cordelia didn't inform you that the limit of your funds had been reached?" the Marquess asked, his voice amiable.

Hearing the warning in his voice, Gabrielle faltered, for just a moment.

"Well, I just thought she'd put aside some of her items," Gabrielle said, fluttering her eyelashes at Philip. She knew it made her look even younger and more innocent than she was. "After all, with my debut imminent, there are certain necessities to success. I know Cordelia agrees with me that I must appear to my best advantage. She was so generous today with providing me everything I needed, I didn't expect her to quibble over such a small matter. After all, even if we did exceed our allowance, it wasn't by very much."

"From now on, you and Lady Dunbury will have separate allowances," his slight emphasis on her title made it clear that he didn't approve of Gabrielle's use of her name. "Your extra purchases today will be deducted from that allowance, and if you continue to exceed your limit, eventually you will reach a month when you have no allowance at all. You will also be disciplined every time you exceed your limit, to teach you some constraint. Please stand and bend over the arm of your chair, lift your skirts and present yourself for your punishment."

"What?!" All the color had drained from Gabrielle's face as the Marquess had spoken, until it flushed again at his final order.

His gaze on Gabrielle was implacable. "Position yourself for a spanking. I'm aware that your stepmother informed you of the disciplinary consequences that I intend to uphold in this household. Today you were disobedient of your stepmother, both selfish and extravagant in your purchases, and disrespectful upon your return home. So you will be spanked, and hopefully there will not be a repeat of today."

Practically sputtering, for the first time in her life, Gabrielle looked to her stepmother for support.

"Cordelia! You can't let him - you shouldn't - I..." Gabrielle's voice trailed off as Cordelia's jaw locked into place, and she realized that her stepmother wasn't going to stop any of this. Furious, frightened eyes turned back on Philip. "I'm not a child!"

Even though Cordelia had told Gabrielle that this was possible, she hadn't truly believed it. She certainly hadn't believed Cordelia would actually allow her new husband to beat Gabrielle.

"Then you should not have acted as one. Your spanking is currently at a count of twenty. If you do not get up and put yourself in position, I shall begin adding five swats for each minute that you delay." The ruthless authority in the Marquess' voice made it clear that this was no idle threat. Tears began to spill from Gabrielle's big, green eyes, real tears that had her cheeks and nose turning red, as she looked between her two guardians and seemed to realize that no relief would be forthcoming.

Gabrielle glanced towards the door... but what was the point? There was nowhere she could go, no one she could turn to. None of her relatives would take her in, or they would have done so already. None of them were close relatives anyway. They certainly wouldn't care that her guardian wanted to spank her. She didn't doubt that the Marquess would make her pay for any resistance on her part. Sniffling, she moved around to the side of the chair, staring at it as she tried to scrounge up the motivation to actually place herself over it.

The Marquess provided it.

"Twenty-five."

With a squeak, Gabrielle practically threw herself forward, her stomach landing on the armrest, pushing her bottom into the air. The position was humiliating in the extreme. The last time she'd been punished like this, she'd been a little girl and it had been her Nanny doing the job.

"I hate you," she spat, a sob in her voice as she reached back to lift up her skirts. "I hate you both."

Her stomach roiled as she heard the Marquess moving behind her, her bottom automatically clenching and then unclenching. Fear filled her, followed quickly by shame. How could Cordelia allow this? Tears rolled down her cheeks as she bit her lip to keep her sobs to herself. She might have to do this, but she didn't have to give them the satisfaction of hearing her misery.

"Do not attempt to cover yourself," the Marquess said, his authoritative tone making her shiver. "I do not wish to injure your hands by accident. If you reach back to cover yourself, I'll tie your hands in place to ensure that you hold your position. You will be given twenty swats for your disobedience, selfishness, and disrespect and then another five for dawdling. Do you understand?"

"Yes! I hate you!" It was the last gasp of defiance that she could muster, even as a fine tremor went through her body. Gabrielle was going to die of shame and pain, she was sure of it.

SMACK!

Gabrielle shrieked loudly, her hands instinctively starting to reach back towards her bottom before she abruptly stopped herself. It hurt! It hurt so much more than she could have imagined! The paddle was long enough that it had impacted against both cheeks of her bottom, making her skin spark with pain, like the first licks of flame against her skin.

"That was not included in either count," the Marquess intoned. "You and you alone earned this punishment, and I will not tolerate any disrespect, insults or invocations while you're being disciplined. Do you understand?"

Gabrielle nodded her head, burying her face in her hands. She bit her finger to keep from saying anything, because she knew she would not be able to speak without crying. Damn him! Damn them both!

"Very well. We'll begin. My lady," he said, obviously to Cordelia and not to Gabrielle, "if you would please count the strokes."

Obedient, awful Cordelia. Gabrielle wanted to sneer, except she was feeling too pitiful to even attempt one. She turned her face so that she could see her stepmother and glared at her, wanting her to have to see exactly what she was condoning. Cordelia's face was so pale her skin almost looked translucent, but she didn't speak up to defend Gabrielle. Didn't speak up to stop this.

SMACK!

Despite her determination not to, Gabrielle cried out.

"One." Cordelia's voice came out as a mere whisper, so soft that Gabrielle barely heard her, before her voice strengthened. "One."

SMACK!

Another pathetic cry as the paddle's impact landed against already pink skin. Gabrielle hated that she couldn't keep quiet, but it hurt so much!

"Two."

Gabrielle clenched her fists to keep from reaching back to cover herself as the spanking continued. She couldn't stop crying out. She couldn't stop the spanking. She couldn't do anything but kick and cry and pray for it to soon be over.

The paddle was landing fast and hard, with just enough time between strokes to allow Gabrielle to cry out and then get her breath back. By seven she was crying pitifully and had turned her face away from her stepmother. It was clear that Cordelia was horrified, but she wasn't going to help either. By twelve she was sobbing. At fifteen she tried to cover her bottom and Philip quickly snapped out that, if she didn't remove her hands, he'd tie them down *and* they'd start the count over. She'd sobbed and then brought her hands back up her body, putting her arms beneath her chest as holding them there.

SMACK!

"Sixteen."

Gabrielle wished she'd never added those extra items to her shopping list. Why *hadn't* she stopped? Why hadn't she at least told Cordelia that she'd wanted to add those items? Her stepmother probably would have made some of her own sacrifices… but Gabrielle had wanted to be sneaky. She had wanted to do something without permission, without having to ask. She'd wanted to feel like a real woman, a real person, able to buy a few paltry items without feeling like a beggar. The Marquess was not related to her, his money was not her money, but for a few moment she'd wanted to pretend that nothing had changed… that she could spend what she wished, get what she wanted… and she'd wanted the things that would make her feel more like a lady. Make her feel more comfortable in the capital. Instead, now she was bent over being spanked like a child. Her bottom was burning, it felt swollen and hot and she was sure that she couldn't take anymore.

SMACK!

"Twenty."

"Stop! Please, please, stop, I'm sorry! I'll be good, I promise, I'll-"

SMACK!

"Twe-twenty one," Cordelia stammered out. Gabrielle barely heard her as she screamed into the seat of the chair.

She took in a breath, expecting another blow, but it didn't come and for a moment her heart soared with hope.

"We appreciate the apology, Gabrielle, but that does not mitigate your punishment." The Marquess' voice was firm and unyielding, and Gabrielle's heart broke. "What kind of example would I be setting if I did not follow through with my word?"

SMACK!

"Twenty two."

Gabrielle screamed again, her incoherent begging spilling from her mouth without thinking. Any pride she'd had left was gone – she would do anything to stop the spanking. She was so, so sorry that she'd even gone shopping today. She would never, ever, ever, buy anything without Cordelia's permission again. It wasn't worth it.

As usual, she was not in control of her life, and it was pointless to pretend otherwise.

After the twenty-fifth swat, Gabrielle collapsed against the chair, sobbing piteously, until suddenly her stepmother was there, pulling Gabrielle into her arms. The warmth of her embrace and the need that Gabrielle felt for that comforting contact had her crying even harder. This part of punishment, Gabrielle remembered and didn't hate. Nanny had always held her after a spanking, letting her cry it out. She was shocked to have a positive memory of being punished, even as her bottom throbbed harshly. The fabric of her drawers felt like sandpaper against her sensitive skin.

She'd certainly never been paddled before and the wooden instrument had burned her backside. She cried into Cordelia's shoulder, taking the comfort that she could, clinging to the human contact, completely wrung out and not caring who was providing the comfort.

"You did very well, Gabrielle," the Marquess said, and she could hear the sincerity in his voice. What she couldn't understand was why it made her feel better. Why she suddenly felt warm from the inside out. He had just spanked her! She'd hated every second of it, she'd hated him… and yet she found herself feeling uplifted by his praise. "I'm very impressed at how well you took your first spanking."

Cordelia rubbed Gabrielle's back, making comforting noises as Gabrielle's tears slowed. When Gabrielle felt she had control of herself, she stepped back. She couldn't understand why she wanted comfort from the very people who had just humiliated and punished her. Cordelia had counted out every one of the strokes that the wooden paddle had landed on Gabrielle's buttocks, she had sat there and done nothing while Gabrielle cried and begged for it to stop… but now Gabrielle wanted her hugs and she'd warmed to the Marquess' praise. She'd felt so alone and abandoned during the spanking and now she felt brutally confused by the sudden change in her emotions.

What was wrong with her?

"Do you have anything you'd like to say to Lady Dunbury?" Philip asked, his voice prodding.

"Please, I'd prefer it if she call me Cordelia," Cordelia said, looking up at the Marquess earnestly. "I've always thought of Gabrielle as more of a younger sister than anything else, and I would like that to continue."

"Very well."

More confused than ever, Gabrielle felt truly contrite. Did Cordelia actually see her as a younger sister? She'd always felt that Cordelia tolerated her, felt responsible for her… but a younger sister was more than that. Gabrielle didn't know how to feel anymore.

"I'm sorry for my behavior today," she said softly, knowing it was expected of her, wanting to get away from the room so that she could allow her emotions to settle. Try to discern why she felt the way she did. "It won't happen again." That was certainly true. She would never go behind Cordelia's back like that ever again. The price wasn't worth it.

As Gabrielle swayed slightly on her feet, the Marquess called Molly back to return Gabrielle to her room. She clung to the maid on the way back to the room, even more thankful it was Molly and not Bonnie who was assisting her.

"It's alright, Miss," Molly said sympathetically. "The worst is over now."

"Could you hear everything?" Gabrielle asked hoarsely, her throat feeling sore from all the screaming and crying she'd done.

Molly hesitated, then patted Gabrielle's hand. "Yes Miss, but no one else was in the hall, and I won't tell nobody neither."

"Thank you."

"Let's get you into bed... would you like my girls to visit with you tomorrow?"

"Maybe." She loved spending time with Molly's daughters, they were sweethearts at eight and ten and loved practicing doing Gabrielle's hair, but she didn't know if she'd be up to any visitors tomorrow. Her bottom burned and her emotions were roiling.

On one hand, she was furious that Cordelia had allowed the Marquess to spank her. On the other, she knew that there was truly nothing Cordelia could have done to stop him. She was still flummoxed by Cordelia's assertion that she saw Gabrielle as a sister, and bewildered by her happiness that the Marquess had complimented her after the punishment, even as she was enraged at him for delivering it.

At breakfast the next day, Gabrielle's confusion cleared. The Marquess gave Cordelia everything she'd wanted but hadn't purchased yesterday. There was nothing for Gabrielle but hard looks and a complete lack of sympathy as she squirmed uncomfortably in her chair. Although her bottom had stopped burning, the deeper soreness still lingered, reminding her that yesterday she'd been disciplined... but then she'd also been cared for, comforted, and praised.

Today she was ignored, brushed aside, and unwanted in their happy little lovefest breakfast. So she ran to her room, unable to endure watching another minute of Cordelia fawning over her gifts while the Marquess stared at her like she was the only woman in the world. Gabrielle couldn't remember anyone ever looking at her that way. Not even her own father. Although, he'd had a very similar expression whenever he'd looked at one of his wives, including Cordelia. Then, it was because they held the hope for his future, the hope to fulfill his desire to have a precious son. Now, the Marquess looked at Cordelia in a similar way, but it was different as well… as if she was his hope for the future and yet, something more too. It made Gabrielle's heart ache with jealousy, and she'd quit the room before she could let her spite and bitterness lash out and earn her another spanking.

She was learning, she thought bitterly, as she threw herself onto her bed, wallowing in her loneliness. Why she'd thought things might be different this morning, she didn't know. She was still the outsider looking in on other's lives, on other's happiness, the way she'd always been and probably the way she'd always be.

To her shock, Cordelia came to find her after breakfast. She was the last person Gabrielle wanted to see. She hadn't wanted Cordelia to actually witness how upset she was, but Cordelia came in after knocking once, and Gabrielle didn't have time get up off the bed.

With her face buried in the pillow, she felt her temper rising as her supposed personal space was invaded by her stepmother.

"Get out."

"Now, Gabrielle-"

"Get out! I hate you!" Gabrielle finally looked up at Cordelia, her eyes red and swollen from crying and her face streaked with tears. "Why are you even in here? You've gotten everything you want! A husband who gives *you* presents and beats *me*!"

"Gabrielle! He didn't beat you," Cordelia said, astonished. "I would never let him do such a thing."

"You sat there and watched while he spanked me!"

"You earned that spanking," Cordelia said, and Gabrielle didn't even care if Cordelia was right. Cordelia was the one who had gotten her into trouble anyway. If she'd just kept quiet and not argued about the package, none of this would have happened. "And Philip is letting you keep everything you bought, which is very generous of him."

"Oh, just get out. I knew you would side with him. I know how much you hate me. You probably enjoyed watching him humiliate me." Gabrielle burst into noisy sobs again and buried her face back in her pillow, rolling away from Cordelia. She wanted to find the deepest, darkest hole in the world and crawl into it and never come out. She hated this house, she hated the Marquess, and she hated Cordelia. She didn't care anymore if either of them liked her.

"I don't hate you, Gabrielle," Cordelia said softly. "I never have. I only want what is best for you. I don't want to see you spanked again, and I didn't want to see it yesterday, but if you earn another spanking, I will be there for it. Not because I enjoy watching it, but so that you aren't alone. Things are going to be different now, but different doesn't have to mean bad."

"Different." Gabrielle snorted, her voice bitter. "Good for you and horrid for me. Just get out, Cordelia. Go away and leave me alone."

Curling into an even tighter ball, Gabrielle didn't know if she felt relieved or even more lonely when Cordelia sighed and stood. Part of her wanted Cordelia to stay and keep trying. Another part of her wanted Cordelia to leave and never come back.

"We'll be going for a ride this afternoon in Hyde Park. Philip wishes to take us out in his landau."

"Lovely," Gabrielle said flatly. "Now leave. Please."

CHAPTER 3

HYDE PARK

"Your eyes sparkle like emeralds when you smile, please, my lady, bestow another upon us!"

Gabrielle couldn't help but laugh at the outrageous antics of the young men flocked around the carriage. Her bottom was still tender, even on the cushioned seats of the carriage, but she didn't care. This was... lovely. The difference between this morning and this afternoon was like a paste gem to a real one. One looked well enough, but it was false and spotted, while the other was real and true and beautiful.

The day was beautiful, the lords and ladies decorated the park like brightly colored birds, and the young gentlemen were paying attention to her. *Her.* Not Cordelia, who was seated right next to her. Wearing her new green walking gown and matching hat, Gabrielle knew that she looked lovely, although she didn't think she would ever tire of hearing the gentlemen tell her so. Even better, they didn't seem to require her to converse with them, so she needn't fear saying the wrong thing. Just ask a few leading questions and they were more than happy to regale her on any topic, allowing her to nod and laugh, while quietly observing how other ladies handled themselves.

"You shouldn't indulge them so much, they'll become greedy," said Lady Spencer, teasingly. The beautiful, buxom brunette had been introduced, along with her husband, the Earl of Spencer, and had immediately been drawn to Gabrielle's side. Her warm brown eyes were utterly guileless, and Gabrielle had immediately felt comfortable with her. Lord and Lady Petersham, who had arrived with the Spencers, were more interested in speaking with Cordelia and the Marquess. Gabrielle didn't mind, she wasn't particularly fond of Irene and she had a feeling it was mutual.

"Lady Spencer, do not encourage her cruelty," one of the gentlemen, a handsome man with sandy blond hair who had been introduced as Lord Eckeridge, pleaded. "Miss Astley, we cannot help but be greedy for sights of such beauty, it would be a crime to hide your smiles away from the world."

"Then you must tell me things to make me smile," Gabrielle said coyly, although her lips were still curved as she said it.

Some part of her wondered how she could be so happy, when the cheeks of her bottom were still sore from being spanked and when she'd been so angry this morning... she glanced over at the Marquess, and to her shock, saw him looking at her with something like approval. Warmth blossomed in her chest, although she tried to push it down.

Gabrielle's feelings towards the Marquess were unsettled to say the least. She was embarrassed, infuriated, but she was also thrilled that he'd just looked at her with approval. This morning she'd been sure he hated her, that she would never be happy, and that her life was going to be constant misery from that point onward.

And so far it was the best afternoon of her life.

She was still brutally confused by it all, but she was also determined to enjoy herself while she could. So she pushed away all her conflicting thoughts, turned her back on the Marquess and Cordelia, and focused on the gentlemen vying for her attentions, and the friendly regard of the Countess of Spencer. It was truly a lovely afternoon.

~

DINNER AT DUNBURY HOUSE

This was dreadful. Felix wondered if he was losing his mind. Unable to stay away, he'd come to Dunbury House for dinner. He hadn't been able to think of anything but Miss Astley and Cordelia; worried that both thought him a brute. Now it was quite clear that Cordelia didn't think so, but Miss Astley was certainly holding a grudge.

No matter what words came out of his mouth, somehow they were always the wrong ones... and yet, there was something satisfying about prodding Gabrielle and watching her smolder. Seeing any kind of passionate response flaring up in her bright green eyes just spurred him forward... and the only way he received that response was by being his most charming.

Which made no sense. Most women would hang on his every word - even Cordelia wasn't immune - but not Gabrielle. She was the picture of a well-bred young lady, wearing a cream colored dress that made her skin look like ivory, her light brown hair seem richer in color, and her green eyes even brighter. But then she'd open her mouth - she was sarcastic, witty, and occasionally rude, and for some reason he couldn't help but be fascinated by it. So he directed all of his comments at her, and watched her response to the most innocuous of conversational topics.

"I was at the theater last night," he said, in response to one of Cordelia's questions. "It was quite stimulating. Everyone's already talking about Kean's Shylock." He tilted his head at Gabrielle. "Perhaps you'll be able to see him this Season, Miss Astley."

The fire that lit up her eyes turned them to sparkling emeralds as her fingers tightened on her silverware. Why such a mundane comment would infuriate her, he had no idea, but he'd known it would before he'd said it.

"I think that sounds lovely," Cordelia said, cutting off any response Gabrielle might have made. "I've always wanted to go to the theater."

"Then we shall," Philip said, giving her an indulgent smile before shooting a warning glance at Felix. Felix smiled innocently back at him, but he knew his friend wasn't fooled - Philip knew that Felix was needling Gabrielle on purpose. He just couldn't fathom why or how to stop him, when Felix was doing nothing but making polite conversation. There was going to be an uncomfortable conversation to be had, once the ladies left them to their port, but Felix just couldn't stop himself.

"You should absolutely wear that gown when you do, Miss Astley," he said, taking particular note of the delicate ribbon trim. "Lilac is already the fashionable color of the Season, did you know?"

He could have sworn he heard her growl.

THE LADIES DEPARTED for the drawing room while the footmen brought in the brandy decanter and glasses. Felix felt a tinge of loss as the door shut behind the ladies. There was just something invigorating about verbally sparring with Miss Astley. Unfortunately, Philip was definitely not as amused by their repartee.

"Sorry, old chap," Felix said as he shrugged away Philip's glower. "Something about the girl gets under my skin."

"Well if I can't take you to task for not controlling yourself, how am I supposed to justify doing so to her?" Philip asked irritably.

"I was nothing but charm and civility personified," Felix pointed out.

"Especially after you realized how much it bothered her," Philip retorted dryly.

Felix shrugged. He couldn't help it... he liked seeing her green eyes flash. Was fascinated by the complexities of her personality. It was such a contrast, her almost friendliness with the servants against the way she bristled at a mere compliment from him. If he couldn't inspire her passion in one way, then at least he could have this.

She certainly didn't react that way to anyone else. He'd seen her charming, and now he knew that she had been acting, he'd seen her blank and withdrawn, and he much preferred her honest reactions to him. It was like getting a little glimpse at the real Gabrielle, and he hoped that it would help him figure her out. The fascination he had with her was new and strange to him, and he told himself it was just because she didn't react like women normally did. He really had intended to charm her originally. It occurred to him that he was probably going to have to tender her an apology before she would accept any of his attempts to do so.

Apologizing was not something he was very familiar with. Felix sighed.

~

"I DON'T UNDERSTAND why you think Felix humiliated you," Cordelia said, rubbing her temples.

Gabrielle felt just a small moment of guilt that she was causing Cordelia to have a headache, but that was quickly swept away by the fact that it was Cordelia's fault for having Mr. Hood to dinner anyway. And forcing Gabrielle to join them. Not only had she had to deal with her conflicting emotions about the Marquess, and face him despite her humiliation at his hands, but her lovely day had been ruined the moment she'd seen Mr. Hood's smug face.

His smug, handsome, chiseled face, framed by that glorious black hair.

Her stomach had dipped and then she'd flushed hot, wondering if he knew about the spanking she'd received from the Marquess. They were best friends after all, and Mr. Hood had threatened to spank her before. The way he looked at her, with that dark, knowing gaze, just made her feel even more vulnerable - and more sure that he knew something.

It wasn't fair that such an awful man was so handsome. And he was devilishly handsome in his stark white and black attire, trimmed with gold to set off his dark good looks.

"He was mocking me this entire evening," she seethed, venting her frustration now that she and Cordelia were alone. Thank goodness for the social niceties that sent the ladies to the drawing room after dinner while the men enjoyed their port and cigars. She didn't think she could have stood another second in discussion with the arrogant nodcock. Cynthia had taught her the word nodcock today and it sounded perfect to describe Mr. Hood. "You know very well that he threatened to beat me, but all evening he was prodding me and pointing out all my deficiencies!"

Cordelia gave her an incredulous look, sending Gabrielle's ire even hotter. She dropped her voice in a deft mimicry of Mr. Hood's condescending tones.

"'The balls are absolute crushes, Miss Astley, as I'm sure you'll discover,' 'Lilac is already the fashionable color of the Season, Miss Astley, did you know?' 'Everyone's talking about Kean as Shylock, perhaps you'll be able to see him this Season, Miss Astley.'"

All the things she knew nothing of, and he rubbed her face in it, lording it over her how much more sophisticated and worldly he was. If he wasn't such an arrogant blaggard she would probably have enjoyed hearing about London life from him, but she knew that beside him she must look like a complete ninny with her country ways and ignorance, and she hated that.

"I don't think he was mocking you," Cordelia said, in the tone that meant she thought Gabrielle was being unreasonable, but she wasn't going to mention it, because of course Cordelia was always patient and tolerant and just perfect. No wonder Mr. Hood preferred Cordelia's company to Gabrielle's, even if Cordelia was married to his best friend. "He just wanted to tell us some of the things to do and see in London, and to prepare us for your come-out ball and entrance to the *ton*. He was just trying to help."

"Yes, help the poor, provincial country bumpkins," Gabrielle sneered as the bitterness that always seemed to lay around her heart swelled up. Of course the only attention she could receive from Mr. Hood was at the Marquess' orders or because she was an object of pity. "Mr. High-and-Mighty Hood to the rescue. Of course you would think that, he was practically falling all over you, I was shocked that Dunbury allowed it. All three of you make me sick. I'm going to my room, I can't stand one more minute with any of you."

The truth was, she thought miserably as she stomped away, she couldn't stand one more minute of being in Mr. Hood's presence while wondering what he truly thought of her. The gentlemen this afternoon, in the Park, had all been content to talk about themselves, allowing her to listen, without having to contribute much in the way of conversation. Mr. Hood seemed determined to engage her, which only highlighted how very little she knew about London and the world at large… if he'd only been willing to speak without requiring a response, she would have been much more comfortable.

She wished she could be more adept at conversation, but instead her tongue tied and she felt more provincial than ever in his presence. All the while, he kept giving Cordelia admiring glances, as she had no problem conversing with him. It had made Gabrielle feel very much on the outside again, like a child pressing her nose to a candy shoppe, knowing that the treats within were far out of her reach.

Gabrielle's Come Out

On the Marquess' arm, heading towards the ballroom, Gabrielle felt like a princess. This was her night - finally her night! - and everything was going to be perfect.

In the days leading up to the ball, everything had not been perfect... she'd been dizzy with doubts, burdened with anxiety, and had driven Cordelia round the bend, until she'd almost been spanked by the Marquess for it. Cordelia had intervened though, and Gabrielle had been both grateful and strangely… not. Part of her almost wished that she had been spanked, just so she could have an excuse to scream out all the nerves that had taken up residence in her body.

Still, the threat had been enough to have her toeing the line immediately after that. She just wanted her come-out to be perfect.

Tonight at dinner she'd been seated with Viscount Petersham and

Lord Hyde, with Lady Spencer (who had invited Gabrielle to call her Cynthia) close enough to speak with, and the conversation had been wonderful. Of course, she'd been very aware of Mr. Hood, further down the table's length, charming the ladies left and right, but she'd mostly been able to ignore his obnoxious presence. For the first time, everything she'd learned about horses and hounds, in order to please her father, actually came of use. Both Lord Hyde and Viscount Petersham seemed delighted with her interest and regaled her with stories, encouraging her input and questions. Not only that, but the Marquess had seemed pleased with her as well and she finished the dinner already feeling like a glowing success.

The receiving line had been just as successful. So many guests! All attired gorgeously - although some of the fashions were rather astounding. Gabrielle had never seen so many giant feathers! She was glad that, as a debutante, the fashion didn't call for her to wear either feathers or a turban. They seemed rather silly.

Instead, she was in an ivory gown trimmed with light pink ribbons that brought out the pink in her cheeks. The flounce on the skirt brushed over the floor as she walked, with a lovely swishing noise.

As they approached the ballroom, there was a lone figure standing outside of the doors, waiting. Mr. Hood, looking resplendent in his usual black and white, although he was wearing a dark plum waistcoat - it was so dark it was almost black anyway, so it didn't truly add any color to his attire. The way he looked at her as they approached made her feel rather strange inside. She couldn't fathom what he was thinking. The Marquess slowed his pace as they neared Mr. Hood, raising an eyebrow in question.

"Lady Gabrielle," Mr. Hood said, bowing formally and ignoring the Marquess and Cordelia, his roguish smile doing funny things to the inside of Gabrielle's chest. "You look lovely this evening. I would be honored to claim one of your dances."

"Would you?" she asked, her chin jutting up challengingly. She couldn't think of anything else to say, because she couldn't imagine why he would want to dance with her - or be waiting outside the door to ask her to do so before she'd even entered the ballroom. Some forgotten part of her, some stupidly romantic part of her, wafted up the vain hope that perhaps Cordelia had been correct in saying that Mr. Hood wanted to help. That he hadn't meant to be condescending or cruel. That perhaps, just maybe, he was as interested in her as the gentlemen who had swarmed the carriage at Hyde Park. Yet, the more sensible and realistic part of her couldn't believe that, and so she hid behind a veil of disdain, afraid to let herself hope. Out of the corner of her eye, she could see the Marquess and Cordelia watching - not interfering - and she knew that, as always, she was on her own.

Mr. Hood's dark eyes flashed, but she didn't recognize the emotion. He straightened and held out his hand.

"Your dance card, Lady Gabrielle?" The challenge in his voice was just as clear; he was ordering her to oblige him.

Strangely, it made her heart flutter. She pursed her lips, slowly lifting her arm in front of her, but letting the card and pencil dangle down instead of handing them to him. Quick as a wink, Mr. Hood snatched both up and scribbled his name down - and then again. She made a protesting noise and tried to pull away, only to freeze at his triumphant smile.

Was he triumphant because he'd gotten one over her? Or because he truly wanted to dance with her? If he was still mocking her...

Her cheeks flushed with emotion as her confusion soared and she clenched her fists, watching Mr. Hood slip away into the ballroom.

"It's a good thing I'm already opening the dancing with you," the Marquess said, taking up her hand again and giving her an encouraging smile. Gabrielle blinked, looking up at him, and smiled tremulously back. "Otherwise I might not get a turn."

He looked down at her approvingly and Gabrielle felt her cheeks flush for a different reason. The Marquess was pleased with her! Cordelia was smiling at her as well. Perhaps Mr. Hood hadn't been mocking her after all. Surely the Marquess and Cordelia wouldn't look so calm if he had been.

~

"You dance very well," Mr. Hood said, smiling down at her.

Gabrielle blinked. The entire first dance they hadn't spoken at all - although, the movements of that particular dance didn't encourage conversation either - and now, on their second dance, he'd been silent up to this point. Now he seemed surprised.

Her mouth firmed. "For a country mouse, you mean."

"No." He frowned down at her.

"Did you not expect me to dance well?" she prodded, giving him a haughty look.

His black eyes seemed to grow even darker. "Of course I did... why would you even ask that?"

"You were the one who commented on it."

"I was trying to compliment you." He growled the words and Gabrielle eyed him warily. He looked over at the court of young men waiting for her to finish dancing with him. "You don't seem to mind when any of them compliment you."

"Perhaps they're better at it," she replied tartly.

Impudent baggage. And yet... he was enjoying himself much more than when he was dancing with a young lady who did nothing but simper at him and lap up his flattery.

"Perhaps you are just incapable of taking a true compliment, instead of the empty flattery of buffoons," he retorted. She stiffened, eyes flashing, which immediately stirred him. It was wrong to enjoy her temper the way he did, but, god help him, he liked it.

"They aren't buffoons and it's not empty flattery," she said through gritted teeth. She was trying to keep a smile on her face, but it looked more like she was baring her teeth at him. The smile that spread across his own face was much more sincere.

"They are absolutely buffoons... I'm much more interesting. And sincere. I sincerely conclude that you dance divinely."

"You would know," she said darkly. "After all, I'm sure you've done quite a bit of *dancing*."

"Jealous?"

The look she gave him made it clear she thought he was stark raving mad. "What?"

Damn, he'd misread that entirely. He'd thought she was referring to the other young ladies he'd danced with this evening, but apparently she'd been speaking of something else entirely. He just couldn't imagine what, and looked at her... this time with sincere bafflement. Then he sighed. As invigorating as verbally sparring with her was, he would like to actually get to know her better. She was so closed off, and she obviously didn't like speaking to him. He was going to have to do something he'd really hoped to avoid.

"Gabrielle - "

"Lady Gabrielle." Her eyes sparked as she reminded him that she hadn't given him leave to use her Christian name.

"Well you may call me Felix," he snapped back. He took a deep breath. "Lady Gabrielle, I would like to apologize for the, ah, the way I spoke to you at your stepmother's wedding. I was out of bounds."

She blinked, her lips parting in astonishment, and he couldn't help but wonder how she'd react if he bent over and kissed them.

The music ended and he wanted to curse.

His lips firmed as he took her hand to lead her back to her court. As they walked, she looked up at him through her lashes.

"Apology accepted," she murmured. "You may call me Gabrielle, if you like."

Somewhat shaken by Mr. Hood's – Felix's - apology, as it had been entirely unexpected, Gabrielle went to the retiring room to compose herself. Dancing with him had been much more interesting than dancing with any of the other young men she'd spent time with this evening. He was a wonderful dancer, very strong and sure-footed, and it was impossible not to realize that being held in his arms felt very different from being held in anyone else's.

She couldn't help but wonder if she had been more sensitive to some of his comments, as Cordelia had accused her of. Tonight, she'd thought he'd been mocking her when he'd complimented her dancing – after all, he'd been dancing all evening with women who were much more graceful and sophisticated than her, and obviously used to gracing the parties of the *ton*. Then he'd apologized and she'd started to think that perhaps Cordelia had been right; perhaps he'd been sincere in his statements instead of mocking.

"Hello again." The bright greeting distracted Gabrielle, making her blink.

Immediately she curtsied. "Lady Arabella."

While there was no way for Gabrielle to have remembered everyone who passed through the receiving line, certain names and faces stood out. Lady Arabella was the Duke of Manchester's sister, and a stand-out beauty with her elegantly coiffed brown hair and matching brown eyes. She had a creamy complexion that was enhanced by the pink dress she was wearing and the pink jewels sparkling around her throat.

"Oh please, don't do that," Arabella said, waving her hand as she came further into the room. She turned to peer into the same mirror that Gabrielle had been staring blindly into, inspecting her outfit. "I don't stand on ceremony, not like my brother. He's a bit stuffy, if you hadn't noticed."

A smile immediately pushed onto Gabrielle's face. Arabella reminded her immediately of Cynthia, with a warm friendliness that was both unexpected and very welcome.

"So is my guardian, no wonder they seemed to like each other," Gabrielle mused. The other young woman immediately grinned, turning to Gabrielle and putting out her hands. Automatically, Gabrielle raised her own to clasp them.

"I knew I was going to like you," Arabella said, gleefully. "So many of the other misses are such little ninnies, it's as if they have no personality. I've said that exact same thing to four other debutantes and all four of them immediately fell over themselves trying to defend my brother without insulting me." She rolled her dark eyes.

"Why would they do that?" Gabrielle immediately understood that

Arabella had been testing her, but she didn't mind. A Duke's sister probably had all sorts of people trying to befriend her; Gabrielle didn't entirely understand why she was being singled out for special treatment by Arabella, but she appreciated it.

"Because they don't want me to ever tell my brother that they'd even hinted at saying something negative about him," Arabella said blithely. She snorted. "As if I'd ever recommend one of those ninnies to him." Cocking her head, she raised one eyebrow. "Are you interested in a Duke for a husband?"

"Not if he's anything like the Marquess," Gabrielle said, and then slapped one of her hands over her mouth. She hadn't meant to say that, but Arabella just laughed and tugged on the hand she was still holding, linking her arm through Gabrielle's.

"We're going to be *very* good friends, I can already tell."

A rush of happiness went through Gabrielle as she followed Arabella back into the ballroom. Tonight was easily the best night of her life. It was too bad she'd already had two dances with Mr. Hood; he wouldn't ask for a third as two was most a couple could dance without practically announcing their engagement. If only he'd apologized during the first dance, then the night would have been perfect.

In between sets, Felix found himself drawn back to Gabrielle's little court again and again. It had doubled in size, after she'd returned from the retiring room with the Duke of Manchester's sister. The two of them were a pretty pair, and – with their respective dowries – worth a small fortune. It was no wonder that they drew the majority of the men's attention.

Yet, for once, Gabrielle always had a smile for him. He wished they could dance again, but he'd already had his second turn with her about the floor. A third dance would have signaled to the *ton* at large that he was serious in his pursuit of her, and, to be perfectly frank, he wasn't entirely sure he was ready to take that step yet.

However, he did enjoy that she was finally smiling at him and conversing with him, without bristling at every small thing he said. Still, he couldn't help teasing her on occasion, just to watch her eyes flash.

When Lord Eckeridge took over the conversation, extolling the virtues of visiting Paris to a wide-eyed Gabrielle, Felix couldn't help but step in, knowing that Eckeridge's explorations of the Continent were fairly limited. It wasn't that he was threatened by Eckeridge, but he didn't really like the way Gabrielle was staring up at the man like he was the most interesting man in the world. Eckeridge wasn't even all that well traveled.

"Ah, but if you want truly unique sights, Italy is the place to go," he said, interjecting smoothly between Eckeridge's transports about Versailles. Gabrielle turned to him, eyes alight with interest, and he smiled down at her. "Paris is beautiful, but not all that different from London when everything is said and done. Nothing compares to the frescoes in Florence or the canals of Venice; there's nothing else like them in all the world."

Eckeridge scowled, obviously realizing he'd lost Gabrielle's interest, and Felix grinned with triumph as she leaned towards him, lips slightly parted, as if ready for a kiss. Her simple joy at just hearing about far off places was rather endearing. She was so fresh and innocent in some ways; it made him recall all sorts of details that he'd barely paid mind to when he'd actually been on location, just to see her reaction to his descriptions.

When the evening ended, he felt rather pleased with himself. Not only had she accepted his apology, but he rather thought that he'd outshone all her other earnest suitors.

THE BALL WAS a roaring success and so was Gabrielle; that was evident from all the bouquets that appeared the morning after. She was flush with excitement, as bouquet after bouquet appeared, each with a handwritten card as well as a message within the flowers themselves. By the time the last delivery had been made, in early afternoon, the flowers had completely filled the drawing room.

So when the last card wasn't from the supposedly apologetic Mr. Hood, Gabrielle told herself she didn't care. Not even a bit.

Whatever she'd hoped for after his apology and his attention afterwards, she'd obviously made up in her head. There was no reason to feel disappointed; after all, look at all the lovely flowers she'd received from gentlemen who *were* interested in her.

CHAPTER 4

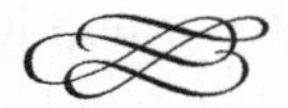

Watching Gabrielle taking yet another turn around the dance floor with another young fortune-hunter, Felix frowned. She'd attracted quite a bit of attention at her come-out, which he supposed was only to be expected. She was beautiful, well-dowered, well-connected, and wonderfully charming when she wanted to be.

For some reason, she just didn't seem to want to be with him. At first he couldn't figure out why she was ignoring him for the rest of the young men that had gathered around her – since he was the only one singled out for such treatment. Then as she'd raved about the flowers that each man had sent her following her come-out, thanking them prettily in turn, he'd realized his blunder.

Well, he'd never liked being part of a crowd anyway.

But he hadn't meant to hurt her feelings either. Regardless, there was nothing to be done about it now. He wasn't in the habit of courting young debutantes – ever – and so it wasn't surprising that he'd made a misstep. He'd been trying to make up for it with their dances, but she held herself back from him there too, only making the bare minimum of conversation. Should he apologize again? Or would pointing out that he was cognizant of his misstep only exacerbate the situation?

"Booth, eh?" Philip asked, coming up beside Felix and frowning as the young Mr. Booth made Gabrielle laugh. "He's in dun territory."

"This is his first dance with her and she's shown him no inclination," Felix said calmly. While he didn't like Booth, he wasn't overly concerned about him either. The man was not well-skilled at subterfuge, not like some of the impoverished rakes that Gabrielle had also attracted. They didn't approach, not with Philip and his cousins, as well as Felix and his brothers, beside Gabrielle's friend Arabella and *her* brothers… but they circled. Like sharks just waiting at a chance to bite into some tasty prey.

"Is there anyone she seems interested in?"

Felix shook his head, thankful for that. The only gentleman who received any kind of significant difference in behavior was himself, and it was not in a positive manner.

"Eckeridge is trying hard though, I think he might actually be smitten – although I doubt he'd be quite so interested without her dowry. He's not up the River Tick yet, but if he doesn't stay out of the gambling houses, he will be soon. Foster and Rothingham are also well caught, they rarely leave her side."

"Foster's not so bad," Philip mused, and Felix had to restrain himself from shouting the idea down. Foster wasn't so bad, he just wasn't right for Gabrielle. She wouldn't be able to run over him exactly, but she wouldn't need to; the man loved to indulge his ladies. Felix had no doubt that his wife wouldn't lack for anything material, although he also doubted Gabrielle would be willing to share her husband with several mistresses. If Felix was her husband, he sure as hell wouldn't have a woman on the side.

In fact, he hadn't had an interest in any other woman since meeting her. It was damned frustrating… but it was also worthwhile. He'd seen the way Philip's, Petersham's, and Hyde's marriages worked; now that the thought of marriage seemed to have burrowed into his brain, he was coming to realize that he wanted to be similarly situated. Just being wed to an attractive woman whom he could discipline as he saw fit wasn't enough; he wanted her to want to submit to him, to be faithful to him, and to love him. He wanted the loyalty that he saw the others' wives give them, and the satisfaction they obviously received from their unions.

"Rothingham would be better," Felix said. He was at least the type who would be faithful, and while he did need to marry a lady with a large dowry, he was a good sort of fellow. Certainly better suited to Gabrielle's temperament than Foster. "He's good husband material and a calm sort of fellow, Gabrielle's dramatics would barely touch him."

"Good, good. Thanks for taking care of her, Felix," Philip said, clapping his hand to Felix's shoulder before a wicked grin crossed his face. "Stand guard on Gabrielle for a bit? I'm ah... going to go see if my wife would like to get a breath of fresh air."

By which he meant he was going to go find Cordelia and drag her off to have his way with her. A pang of envy went through Felix. There had been a time in his life when he could have looked forward to that as well. Instead, he was now spending his time making sure no one did that to Gabrielle.

Watching his friend go, he didn't notice the glittering green eyes that were boring a hole in the back of his head. It never even occurred to him that the dance had ended and someone might have been listening to their conversation.

The Duke of Richmond's House

Her first kiss left Gabrielle breathless.

In part, because she thought she'd never have one. It was clear that the Marquess wanted her to marry, but at the same time, he'd made it nearly impossible for her to truly be courted. Gabrielle's every movement was tracked, by him, his cousins, and - of course - Mr. Hood. Whom she still determinedly thought of as Mr. Hood, now that she'd realized his attempt at closeness by giving her leave to use his Christian name had meant nothing.

She'd almost been taken in by his apology and his charm until she'd discovered that he was one of her 'guards.' Of course the Marquess had asked his best friend to keep an eye on her for the Season.

It had hurt a great deal, because for a very short time, she'd actually thought that Mr. Hood had been interested in her for her. When she'd realized he wasn't, it had also made clear to her what a little fool she'd been. So she'd thrown herself into the attentions of her suitors, and she'd been quite taken with Mr. Pressen.

He was blonde and tall, slim instead of muscular, and wrote her the most romantic letters. They'd been corresponding for two weeks now and he sent her bouquets daily. He wasn't the only one whom she received daily bouquets from, but off all her suitors he was also the boldest. When they danced, he whispered how he longed to kiss her, to touch her. He excited her with little caresses that no one noticed. It was wrong of them, she knew, but also terribly exciting.

Mostly, his obvious interest helped to balm the wound her childish hopes had suffered in regards to Mr. Hood.

So, with the help of Arabella, who was thrilled by the romantic adventure, Gabrielle had snuck away to meet Mr. Pressen alone, away from the ballroom. They'd been writing back and forth for a while, although he only occasionally approached her in the ballrooms since her guards were ever alert, and she was both flattered and excited by his attentions. Going into a dark room with him seemed like an utterly romantic adventure. While she could still hear the sounds of merriment, the library was utterly deserted but for her and Mr. Pressen.

His lips were firm and gentle, his hands cupping her face, one of them sliding to the back of her neck and making her gasp as his fingers trailed over her collarbone. As she did so, his tongue slid into her mouth, shocking her. He tasted of brandy and chocolate, and she felt her curiosity grow as his tongue stroked hers. This was an entirely new world for her. It wasn't unpleasant, although she didn't quite feel the same excitement that she'd expected to. Since it was her first, of course it wasn't exciting, but it seemed to be missing a certain… spark. Perhaps her imagination had gotten away with her. It was a very nice kiss after all.

The kiss deepened and she moved closer to him, her lips clinging to his as they explored each other's mouths.

When the door slammed open, she nearly bit his tongue.

"Gabrielle!"

"Fe- Mr. Hood!" She gasped out, her heart pounding with the knowledge that she'd just been caught... and also fury at who had interrupted her first, magical kiss. The bounder was standing in the doorway, brow furrowed in fury, eyes ablaze, and with an expression she'd never seen before on his face.

"Ah, Hood," Mr. Pressen rumbled, releasing Gabrielle from his hold and giving him a kind of companionable grin. "Room's taken, as you can see, if you're-"

With a dull roar, Mr. Hood bounded forward, slamming the door shut behind him, looking like the very devil with his black eyes afire. He slammed his fist into Mr. Pressen's jaw, knocking him down with one blow, and Gabrielle clapped her hands over her mouth to smother her scream. She was completely shell shocked as Mr. Hood grabbed her arm and dragged her out to the hallway.

"Mr. Hood-

"Not. One. Word." It sounded like he was forcing the words out through his teeth.

"Please… Felix - "

"Don't you dare call me that right now!"

Gabrielle's lips clamped shut. Damn him, damn him to hell and back for ruining her night. Her kiss. Even worse, she couldn't help but examine him for signs that perhaps he was jealous… that maybe his anger stemmed from something more than duty… but then he just handed her off to the Marquess with a succinct account of "what he'd found," which made her roll her eyes, and then he'd followed them to the carriage, but hadn't gotten in with them. He didn't even said goodbye to her, just to the Marquess and Cordelia.

And on top of all that, she already knew she was going to be ending her evening with a spanking.

Bloody hell.

~

WHITE'S

The club was mostly empty; other than Felix and Philip, there were only two other gentlemen present. One was completely engrossed in his newspaper by the fireplace, the other was already passed out and the staff was obviously trying to decide whether or not they should attempt to wake him. Thus was a morning at White's...

Slumped in his chair, Felix studied his friend, who was swirling his brandy in his glass and had been for the past five minutes. He looked down at the glass in his own hand and tried to drum up the inclination to take a sip. Instead, all he could think about was how Gabrielle had looked last night, her lips against Pressen's, her cheeks flushed with happiness. And then how she'd looked at him once she'd gotten over her shock.

He wanted Gabrielle, he truly did, but how long could he go on wanting a woman who did nothing but turn him away? Every time he thought he'd gotten somewhere with her, it turned out he'd actually taken a step or two back. He realized that he'd hurt her feelings when he hadn't sent her flowers after her come out, but dash it all, would she hold that against him forever? While Felix was a master at seduction, it was becoming quite clear to him that he had very little idea how to court a proper young lady. Not that he was courting, Gabrielle, really. He hadn't decided to, yet.

Looking back up at Philip, he saw that his friend was still staring into the depths of his drink.

"I believe you're supposed to sip that, not stare at it. It's not a crystal ball after all," he commented.

Philip sighed. "Even if it were, I don't know that it could help me. Not unless it could show me the perfect husband for Gabrielle and how to get him leg-shackled to her."

Felix winced. He thought he would be a good husband for

Gabrielle - he understood that there was more going on behind those pretty green eyes than she showed the world, and he would be willing to tolerate her temper, while curbing the wildest of her impulses, if she would give him any small sign that she at least didn't despise him.

"I've been thinking," he started to say, and then fell silent. Philip turned towards him, raising an eyebrow as he waited for Felix to continue. Felix ran his finger around the top of his glass, scowling. When he'd first met Gabrielle, he'd joked to Philip that he would take Gabrielle if Philip would include two of his hound pups as a wedding present. At the time, he'd only been half joking. Now... he still felt the same, but Gabrielle's recent behavior had been giving him pause. "I was going to wait till the end of her first season, but I'm still considering offering for Gabrielle."

Well, he'd been thinking about waiting till the end of the Season anyway. If he made an offer. In part because he needed his time to wrap his head round the idea.

"Truly?"

"She's... different." She engaged him like no other woman ever had. Not just because of the challenge she presented, but because he felt that the reward at the end would be more than worth it. The different facets of her personality made him want to figure her out, like she was a puzzle box.

"If by different you mean spoiled and self-involved, although truthfully I don't think that makes her stand out from the other ladies of the *ton*."

Felix immediately felt defensive of Gabrielle. "Because that's not all she is."

"She wants for discipline."

"She also wants for cherishing," Felix said, glaring at Philip. "I'm beginning to agree with your wife, you're too hard on the girl." Gabrielle needed attention. She needed love. She needed to feel like she was desired. After several discussions with Cordelia about how Gabrielle had been treated during her childhood, Felix agreed with her on that. Besides, he couldn't shake that first impression he'd had of Gabrielle, giving those two little girls dresses for their dolls. That wasn't spoiled or self-involved at all. But she certainly was in other ways, so he could understand why Philip thought so.

"I have a lack of patience for those who don't appreciate what they're being given by others. Especially when the one doing the giving is Cordelia," Philip admitted in conciliatory tones.

That was true enough; Gabrielle was not always very pleasant to Cordelia, and it was nearly always undeserved. Of course Philip would feel protective of his wife.

"Understandably."

"And I don't dislike Gabrielle all the time. Her company can be quite enjoyable when she wants to be charming. I'd like her a good deal more if she didn't revert back the second she's not getting her way."

Drumming his fingers on the table, Felix nodded. "She needs her own husband." And her own household. A place that she belonged and that wasn't her stepmother's.

"So offer for her."

"I'm not ready yet." Felix looked away from Philip's probing gaze, marshaling his thoughts. "Marriage is a serious proposition. I want something like what you and Cordelia have. What your cousins have. While I think Gabrielle is attracted to me, I'm not sure that she actually likes me. And after she went off with Pressen last night, I'm not sure how discriminating she is when it comes to attraction."

He wanted her loyalty and her heart, not just her hand in marriage. While he couldn't fault her for being curious, at the same time, he'd been hurt when he'd found her with Pressen. It was one thing for her to ignore him in favor of the flattery of others, since she wasn't paying particular attentions to any of them, but for her to actually encourage one as she had Pressen... He wanted to throw her over his knee and spank the thought of any other man out of her head and then kiss her breathless and pleasure her until the lesson had set.

Felix was well versed in pleasure, and he knew damn well that the wives of the *ton* would often search for it outside of their marriages, and that was exactly what he didn't want. Which was a large part of why Gabrielle's behavior tonight gave him pause. Was she the type who went searching for pleasure, regardless of the source? Or did she have true feelings for Mr. Pressen? If she was just looking for passion, Felix was sure that he could provide and keep her sated, if given the opportunity. But if she truly cared for another man... the key to loyalty, as he'd seen in his peers, was love. So perhaps the question he should truly be asking was – could Gabrielle love him?

CHAPTER 5

JERSEY HOUSE

The social scene wasn't fun anymore, Gabrielle thought sadly. She enjoyed the compliments of her court, but at the same time, she had to suspect everyone's motives. Pressen had disappeared entirely, proving that whatever he'd felt for her, it wasn't strong enough to withstand Mr. Hood's fist. Now she wondered why each man was paying court to her... was it because of her large dowry? Was it because her best friend was a Duke's sister? Was it to impress the Marquess?

Strangely, she didn't hate the Marquess anymore. He wasn't cold, he was just very controlled. And he did care about her, and it didn't seem like it was just because of Cordelia. When he'd spanked her after the incident with Mr. Pressen, his lecture had driven that home. He didn't want her to be ruined – but if she was, she felt sure now that he would still take care of her. In some ways, she almost appreciated that he'd spanked her. If he'd just let the incident go, that would have truly showed he didn't care. They were actually enjoying a better relationship than ever in the aftermath, and he seemed particularly pleased with her normal behavior following her second spanking.

In stark contrast, Mr. Hood no longer danced with her or even attempted an interaction. He just… hovered. Watched her like a hawk. Fulfilled his guard duties. She did her best to ignore him, telling herself that it didn't hurt and she didn't miss him.

Although, if he didn't need to do more than hover to fulfill his duties, then why had he always danced with her and spoken with her before?

It was all too confusing and it hurt too much to think that he might have cared and now he didn't. So she just pretended he wasn't there.

She truly didn't think she could hurt any worse, until she heard the rumors about him and Cordelia.

~

Cordelia leaned into Felix's side, looking at the dance floor, where he'd pretended not to be watching Gabrielle dancing with his eldest brother, Thomas. "Why don't you ask her to dance anymore?"

It didn't surprise Felix that Cordelia had noticed his absence from the social scene and, even more notably, his absence from Gabrielle's dance card even when he did deign to attend. Watching her with her suitors held no joy for him, as she ignored him thoroughly, but he couldn't completely stay away either. At first he'd watched her because he'd needed to know if she had true emotion for Mr. Pressen, but she didn't seem too put out by his disappearance from her circle. Then he'd watched her to see if she had any preferences or if she was looking for passion from any of her other suitors. So far she seemed most circumspect with all of them, but that could have been because of her punishment following her misstep with Pressen.

"She didn't seem to particularly enjoy it when I did."

He glanced down to see Cordelia making a face up at him and he couldn't help but chuckle. Her sunny air might not be as fascinating as Gabrielle's stormy temper, but she could always make him smile.

"Who wouldn't enjoy dancing with you? Did you step on her feet? Check your breath for garlic? Bore her with your conversation?"

"Of course not!" Felix said in his most severe and haughty tones. "I never eat garlic before a ball and my conversation is scintillating." Cordelia laughed, as Felix turned his attention back to the dance floor, where Thomas was escorting Gabrielle back to her court. She looked over at him, meeting his gaze, her eyes flicking over him and then Cordelia, before she abruptly turned away and immediately engaged one of the young buffoons in conversation. "I can't understand why she prefers the company of those other toadies to mine."

"Perhaps she does," Cordelia said slowly, while Felix stewed in his bitter confusion. "Perhaps it's easier to accept their attentions because she doesn't prefer them."

That observation made his head hurt to think about, yet it made a certain kind of sense. How very Gabrielle. He was starting to realize that nothing with her was ever simple or easy, but perhaps that's why he found her so engaging. "You mean, because she does actually care what I think, she prefers their company because it's easier?"

"Well... yes. She's spent most of her life attempting to get the attention of the man she cared most about in the world. By and large, unsuccessfully. Now, in London, she's surrounded by attention and she certainly enjoys it. She's quite hot and cold with Philip. Sometimes it seems like she wants his approval, sometimes is as though she's doing everything she can to make him angry. I think, even though he's not her father, she's begun to look up to him in that manner and she's afraid of being rejected by him as well, so she tries to force it rather than waiting for it to happen on its own. The same could be applied to you."

"She sees me as a father?" Felix was horrified - that was definitely not the route he'd wanted to travel with Gabrielle. Good grief, he wasn't that much older than her! Cordelia gurgled out a laugh, hiding her face behind her fan.

"No, no, I mean, that she actually wants your attention and approval and that frightens her, so she does her best to get your disapproval instead. That way, if you stop paying attention to her, the two of you were at odds anyway, so it won't hurt as much."

"That's very deep, Cordelia."

"Gabrielle isn't shallow, she just acts that way sometimes," Cordelia said defensively. She gave him a repressive look, plainly telling him he should know better.

He smiled down at her. "I know."

HOW COULD a library be so full of books and yet not have a single thing Gabrielle wanted to read? She usually loved Gothic romances, but not a single one appealed. Shakespeare, so often a favorite of hers, seemed uninteresting. She couldn't even drum up any enthusiasm for the collection of travelogues the Marquess had, which she had made it a goal of hers to real all of.

Trailing her fingers over the bindings, she read each title, and dismissed it. Since there were thousands of books in here, she could probably pass quite a bit of time this way.

She should be happy; she was a success in Society, she had friends now, she had suitors… it was everything she ever wanted, so why did she feel so empty? So unhappy?

Mr. Hood's face flashed through her mind and she scowled.

If she were being completely honest with herself, her current melancholy had begun last night. She'd been just starting to think that perhaps Mr. Hood had more of an interest in her than the Marquess' requested guard duties, when she'd overheard the speculation that Mr. Hood and the Marchesse were involved in an affair. While Gabrielle didn't believe it for a moment – Cordelia was in love with the Marquess and she didn't have a disloyal bone in her body – she hadn't been able to dismiss the idea that perhaps Mr. Hood's interest was actually in Cordelia.

Sighing, Gabrielle plunked herself down in one of the huge armchairs that faced the empty fireplace, curling up into the soft seat with a sigh. The problem was… she rather liked Mr. Hood. She didn't want to. It was just, he was so charming, so exciting, and such enjoyable company. Not to mention that he made her heart beat faster just by his mere presence. Which made her feel both defensive and irritable. Pushing him away hadn't gotten rid of him, it just meant that now he didn't talk to her, and that didn't make her feel any better.

"Oh, Philip!" Cordelia's scandalized, excited exclamation preceded the sound of the library door being slammed. Gabrielle peered around the side of the chair, unsure of what was happening, only to be treated to the sight of her stepmother wrapped up in the Marquess' arms. They were kissing, but it didn't look anything like the kiss she'd shared with Mr. Pressen.

This kiss was passionate, deep... it looked like they were locked together at the lips, and Philip's hands were moving all over Cordelia's body in a most possessive and inflammatory way. The couple moved towards the window seat on the other side of the room, kissing all the way. Just seeing it sent a tingle of excitement through Gabrielle's body. As a country girl, she knew the very basics of breeding, but she'd never seen anything quite like this.

"Oh, Philip!" Cordelia repeated as her husband relinquished her lips to begin kissing down the side of her neck, his hand cupping her breast as he bore her down to the window seat, laying her back on the cushions.

Holding her breath, Gabrielle gripped the arm of the chair, not daring to make a single sound. She couldn't – she was too enthralled by the sudden education she was receiving. It was wrong, she knew it was, and yet she couldn't find the motivation to declare her presence. She thought it very likely she would be punished if she were caught witnessing their current activities... and yet she didn't care.

Tugging down the top of Cordelia's gown, the Marquess' head moved over her breast, and Gabrielle's breath caught in her throat as Cordelia arched her back, clutching at the back of her husband's blond hair. From the sounds they were making, it seemed as though the Marquess was actually suckling at Cordelia's breast. Gabrielle's own nipples hardened in response, and she couldn't help but wonder what that felt like... except in her mind the head she would be clutching at was full of dark hair, and her imaginary lover had a striking resemblance to Mr. Hood.

Cordelia moaned as the Marquess switched his attentions to her other breast, leaving her wet nipple pink and pointing in the sunlight. It should have been distasteful, scandalous, but instead Gabrielle felt the strangest tingling in her lower belly and between her legs. The sensation was disturbingly similar to the way she had sometimes felt when Mr. Hood danced with her and held her close to his body.

"Philip! Please… I need you…"

With a groan, the Marquess pulled his head away from Cordelia's breasts, leaving the pink-tipped mounds heaving as she panted for air. He pushed her skirts up and Gabrielle was shocked to see that her stepmother wasn't wearing any kind of undergarments beneath her skirts! The shock at this revelation was so great that she didn't even register the Marquess' movements at first.

Fortunately, the couple was so involved with each other that neither heard Gabrielle's small gasp as she had her first glimpse at a grown male's erect member. While she'd seen babies and small boys playing out in the country, she'd never seen… this. His member jutted out of his body, long and hard and almost angry looking. Gabrielle had been kept away from the fields when the mares were bred, but she knew immediately that this was the male 'sword' to the female's 'sheath.' After all, what else could it be?

He pressed it to Cordelia's womanhood and then shoved in with a violent thrust that had Gabrielle's body throbbing. It looked like it should hurt… but the noises Cordelia was making had nothing to do with pain and everything to do with pleasure. Gabrielle pressed her own hand to the top of her mound, over her skirts, needing the pressure as her body actually felt like it was pulsing there. Pressing against it felt so good that she nearly whimpered, but she knew that the consequences of being caught watching the Marquess and her stepmother like this would be… severe.

The two moved together, moaning and panting, the Marquess' male part piercing Cordelia over and over again. His hand slid between their bodies, rubbing at Cordelia's womanhood, and

Cordelia let out a sharp cry, her back arching upwards. They reached culmination together, holding each other tightly as they rocked, voicing their ecstasy. It was the most shocking and exciting thing that Gabrielle had ever witnessed.

Somehow she remained quiet as they righted themselves. Their loud, almost violent congress was followed by light laughter, soft murmurs, and little caresses. It made Gabrielle ache, because it was – in its own way – so lovely. Strangely, even though she still envied Cordelia, she didn't feel the need to be spiteful to her because of this. Not just because she'd be inviting a spanking, although she knew that to be a contributing factor to her new attitude, but because she knew that Gabrielle's situation wasn't Cordelia's fault. She might want what Cordelia had, but she had to get that for herself.

When her guardians left the library, Gabrielle impatiently waited a dragging ten minutes before she slipped out of the room. Walking felt strange, as though it was rubbing something between her legs, at her womanhood, which felt slick and sensitive. She hurried to her room, where she fell back on her bed and yanked up her own skirts, pressing her hand back over her own mound. The touch was much more potent, much more intimate...

Instinctively she rubbed, and then moaned, and rubbed some more. The vision of the Marquess and Cordelia flashed in her mind, making her movements more frantic as she remembered how they'd looked together... so primal, so animalistic, and yet so arousing to her senses. A new image popped up in her mind, of herself on her back with a lover bending over her, thrusting into her, and he wore Mr. Hood's face.

With a loud cry of shock and ecstasy, Gabrielle reached her first climax. It was to be the first of many that afternoon.

~

MARKHAM HOUSE

Felix still didn't know what to do about Gabrielle. He was still angry over her rendezvous with Mr. Pressen, and yet he was still drawn to her anyway. Lately she'd been blushing so becomingly whenever he tried to speak with her… he hadn't asked her to dance again, as she seemed to have become shy now that she'd been caught. He'd thought she would retain her anger with him longer, but that had obviously given way to embarrassment. Unfortunately, it made her extremely reticent to speak with him, and she obviously preferred the company of her adoring swains to his.

Perhaps it was unsurprising that, when he found himself with a lady admirer a few days later, his ego was in need of some salving. Fresh out of mourning and arrived in London that day, Lady Winchester was quite beautiful, with the same curvy figure as Cordelia and the same rich, dark brown hair that was all the rage this Season. She was dressed in a scandalously low cut blue and cream dress, and he couldn't help but admire her bosom as she thrust it at him, smiling up at him prettily.

"I hope you don't think me too forward, introducing myself," she purred, placing a hand delicately on his arm, obviously not caring if he thought her forward at all. "My friend Lady Roth pointed you out particularly to me as being a wonderful gentleman to reintroduce a lady to the city."

He gave her his practiced rakish smile back, more out of habit than anything else. His affair with Lady Roth had been well over two years ago.

Still, he appreciated that someone wanted to speak with him. Even if it was a randy widow who was just looking for a bit of fun. Perhaps it would do Gabrielle some good to see that he was desirable. He glanced over to see if she had noticed that he'd attracted another lady, but she was stepping out onto the dance floor with Philip and hadn't even glanced in his direction.

"I'll have to thank the lady for remembering me so fondly," he said smoothly. "Unfortunately, my time is rather tied up at the moment."

Lady Winchester pouted up at him with a pretty moue, leaning forward to show off even more of her spectacular bosom. Unfortunately, the sight didn't stir him in the slightest. While her curves were luscious, he desired a more modest set, which was currently dancing with her guardian. Gabrielle and Philip spun around the floor. He was glad that the two had become closer; it was obvious that Philip had started to dote on her – not out of responsibility, but out of actual affection.

More proof that Gabrielle could be wonderfully charming when she chose, considering how Philip had felt about her at first. Although, if he were being perfectly honest with himself, he rather liked her broody and scowling at him. She played at being charming with quite a few of her suitors; with him, she was always real. Even if she was testy, he treasured that glimpse into the truth of her.

Although, he could also tell that she was sincerely sweet with Philip now. And with his brothers, for that matter (and the wretches adored her in return). Just not with him.

"Perhaps we could schedule a time to rendezvous at a later hour," Lady Winchester said, with what she obviously thought was an attractive simper.

For a moment, Felix truly considered it. Even though he didn't find her particularly appealing, he was so frustrated… but no. While she obviously just wanted a bedroom affair, it still wouldn't be fair to use her while another woman was planted so firmly in his mind. And, if he did decide to pursue a true courtship with Gabrielle, it would put him in an even worse position if she were to overhear any gossip about him and another woman. It was one thing to try and draw her attention with a flirtation, quite another to start up an actual affair.

He needed to make a decision – was he going to pursue Gabrielle or not? Remaining on the fence was doing him no favors, as the other men around her pressed their suits while he stayed aloof. Felix sighed inwardly. He was no dab hand at courting debutantes, and he knew that he had bungled things with Gabrielle more than once, but he couldn't quite let go of the hope that perhaps the spark between them could be fanned to a flame.

Smiling down at Lady Winchester, he put her hand on his arm. "My apologies, my lady, but I truly am unable to assist you. However, I think I should introduce you to my brother, Walter."

~

FEELING SICK INSIDE, Gabrielle couldn't even look at the corner of the ballroom where Mr. Hood was having an intimate conversation with a woman who looked just like Cordelia. Same figure, same hair, and from a distance, even her facial features weren't too dissimilar.

All the gossip she'd been overhearing poured through her brain, every sentence and suggestive tidbit, every tittering laugh and muffled giggle that the *ton* had spoken of about Mr. Hood and Cordelia. Gabrielle had brushed it off, because she knew without a doubt that Cordelia would never betray Philip. She loved Philip, with all her heart and soul, and Philip returned that regard. The obvious closeness of Cordelia and Mr. Hood had still grated, however.

He danced attendance constantly on Cordelia, even though he'd been hovering about but not speaking to Gabrielle for days. It had made her jealous, but not like this... not like the sharp, biting pain that was clawing its way out of her stomach. Somehow, despite how much she'd disliked him at first, despite the way he always verbally prodded and poked at her until she bristled like a boar, she'd actually come to very much like him. She'd enjoyed the way he always talked with and danced with her, no matter what she'd done to push him away.

Mr. Pressen had been the last straw, but Gabrielle had still held onto a small hope that perhaps Mr. Hood would move past it and return to his former ways. His constant attentions and the way he ignored her attempts to build up a wall between them. She'd never had to pretend with him, rarely curbed her tongue, and yet he'd always come back for more.

Now it looked like there was no hope for that. He'd found a replacement for Cordelia – and it suddenly made sense why he'd clung to Gabrielle's skirts for so long. It had given him all the excuse he'd needed to remain close to her stepmother… now he was having a flirtation with a woman that resembled Cordelia so closely that they could easily be mistaken for each other at first glance. Now that woman would be receiving his undivided attention, his unrelenting company, his witty repartee, and his teasing jabs.

It always came back to Cordelia, didn't it?

Even if he tired of the woman, he would come back to Cordelia too. Because she was the original. Everyone wanted Cordelia, no one wanted Gabrielle. Why hadn't she learned that yet?

Apparently, some small part of her had been stupid enough to hope for more.

She had to get out of Cordelia's and the Marquess' house. She couldn't do it anymore, not knowing this. Somehow, Mr. Hood had wormed his way into her life and she'd allowed him to, despite the way she'd pushed him away… he'd fooled her into hoping that perhaps he was there for her and she'd fallen. Maybe not in love, but certainly she'd become more attached to him than she'd realized until now. She didn't want to give him up, but she wasn't quite enough of a fool to pine after him either.

It didn't matter who she married anymore, she just knew she couldn't remain where she was – always an outsider looking in on everyone else's happiness. Perhaps she would never find her own happiness, but she didn't have to have her face rubbed in everyone else's.

~

SURREY HOUSE

Lady Winchester was becoming a problem.

Felix had introduced her to all the handsome rakes he knew, any of which would be happy to take her on, but for some reason she continued to cling to him. He was bearing it up as politely as he could, but he'd decided to focus on Gabrielle and now the woman was actively hindering him. Especially because her attentions had not gone unnoticed. Philip had informed him that Gabrielle had been jealous, and he'd caught her looking at him more than once since then.

It was the most hope he'd had in ages when it came to her. Perhaps the time spent apart had been for the best – he'd realized that he truly did want to court her, and she seemed to have been disturbed by his absence, giving him hope that she felt something for him too. Certainly she wasn't as indifferent to him as she sometimes pretended.

If only he could foist the blasted widow onto someone else, he could begin wooing Gabrielle in earnest. As it was, he didn't want to go anywhere near Gabrielle with the widow hanging off his arm – she wasn't exactly discreet with her seduction, no matter who was listening. While it might make Gabrielle jealous, she was the type to respond in kind, and he had no desire to torture himself with that.

"This ball is rather boring," Lady Winchester said with a sigh, fanning herself. Tonight she was clad in a gown of gold and red, with an even lower bust line than before. If her bust line kept creeping down in this manner, eventually she'd be showing her nipples to the entire *ton*. There were men actually drooling over her – why was she so damned attached to him? "Perhaps we could go somewhere else more… lively."

Her hand brushed over his thigh and Felix shifted away, clenching his jaw.

As a gentleman, it was his responsibility to ensure the lady enjoyed her evening. However, there was only so far he was willing to go, especially since he hadn't offered himself as an escort to the lady in question. In fact, at first he'd been relieved that she didn't appear at Surrey House and he'd had hopes she'd gone to one of the other events on offer that evening. He'd been all set to ask Gabrielle to dance when Lady Winchester had appeared out of nowhere.

Sighing, he shook his head. "I'm sorry my lady, but my presence is required here. Perhaps I could find you another escort."

She pouted. Felix was becoming heartily tired of her pouts. "But Felix-"

Gaze skimming over the ballroom, Felix went suddenly rigid. Gabrielle was dancing with Viscount Fenworth – a complete cad whose desperate need for a well-dowered bride was widely known. How the hell had that happened? Arabella's brother, the Duke of Manchester, had been standing with Arabella and Gabrielle, and the man would never have allowed Fenworth near either of them normally.

He brushed Lady Winchester's hand away. Enough was enough. "Excuse me," he said coldly, interrupting whatever inane suggestion she was making. The lady made a scandalized sound as he quickly moved away, heading toward the circle of suitors where Manchester was still standing with Arabella. The Duke was an imposing figure, with dark brown hair and eyes, standing several inches taller than most of the men in the room. He was young to the title, but he wore it with confidence, and had the kind of confident aura that his male peers aspired to but never quite achieved. He too was scowling at the couple dancing together. After all, Philip had made a kind of arrangement with Manchester – everyone watched over both ladies. It made things easier.

Which meant that Manchester would feel responsible for Gabrielle's current dance partner.

"My apologies," Manchester said, when Felix reached him. "My sister was speaking to me; I only turned my attention away for a few moments and Fenworth swooped in."

"Oh pish," Arabella said, smacking her fan against Manchester's arm. "You're all alarmists. Fenworth's hardly going to do anything on the dance floor in the middle of a ball."

"It's not here that we're worried about," Felix said grimly. If Fenworth got Gabrielle outside or alone, even for a moment... He looked at Manchester. "You're fine here with Arabella?"

Manchester nodded. "Hyde and Spencer are by the refreshments table and my brother is in the card room."

Nodding his thanks, Felix went to round up reinforcements. Fenworth might have gotten Gabrielle to dance with him, but that was as far as they'd be going. He wouldn't be given the chance to leave the room with her.

~

"AGREED?"

"Agreed." Gabrielle smiled at the Viscount. "Tomorrow then."

The Viscount smiled back at her, putting her in mind of a snake. She wished she had another suitor that would be willing to move as quickly as Viscount Fenworth... he was not her favorite male, but he wasn't so terrible either. Young, handsome, charming when he wanted to be, and he needed her dowry as quickly as possible. Which meant that he was willing to do things quickly.

Now that she'd decided she wanted out, Gabrielle wanted it to happen as quickly as possible. She didn't think she could stand any more balls where she had to watch Cordelia's look-a-like paired up with Mr. Hood. Her plan was as simple as she could make it, but with all the guards she had, it was also necessarily a bit complex.

Gabrielle couldn't help but sigh as the Viscount led her back to her circle where Arabella's brother, the Marquess, and Mr. Hood – thankfully without his woman – were all waiting, scowling at her and Fenworth. Cordelia and the Marquess must have just returned from wherever they'd snuck off to. They did that quite a lot during the balls. She'd spotted the rest of their friends around the room, blocking all exits in case Fenworth decided to try and run off with her in the middle of a ball.

If only they knew.

CHAPTER 6

It all went off beautifully at first, just as Gabrielle had hoped.

Arabella did her first part, trodding clumsily on Cordelia's hem and tearing it. Off to the retiring room Cordelia went, with Lady Hyde, to make the necessary repairs.

A few minutes later, at his post by the garden door, Lord Hyde was approached by a footman with a rather titillating note, in his wife's handwriting, asking him to come meet her for a clandestine rendezvous. Seeing the Marquess of Dunbury, the Duke of Manchester and the ever-present Mr. Hood still standing with Lady Gabrielle and Lady Arabella, he decided there was no harm in going to meet his wife.

At about the same time as Lord Hyde was heading towards the house's library, a similar note was brought to the Marquess of Dunbury by a different footman. Aroused and incited by the words, the Marquess grinned at how far his little Cordelia had come since they'd wed. Excusing himself, assured that the ladies were still sufficiently chaperoned (especially as this ball seemed particularly low on rakes hovering about), Philip hurried towards the morning room the note had indicated his wife would be waiting for him in.

No sooner had he exited the ballroom, than a delighted Lady Winchester approached and practically threw herself on Felix, causing a small stir. Simultaneously, Arabella had signaled to a group of young ladies that she told her brother she "particularly wanted him to meet." All five young ladies were cousins, blonde, blue-eyed, rather shrill, and overjoyed at the prospect of meeting not just a Duke, but such a singularly *handsome* Duke. The horrified nobleman found himself suddenly surrounded by the bevy of blonde beauties, all chattering to him at once.

It had been remarkably easy. All she'd had to do was imitate some handwriting and have the notes prepared beforehand. She'd left them in a vase by the entrance for Fenworth to pick up and deliver to the footmen, who took them to the Marquess and Lady Hyde. He'd also dropped a word in Lady Winchester's ear – that was the part of the plan that Gabrielle hated the most, but it was necessary to succeed.

Since it was fairly early in the evening, the rakes were not yet out in force and so the guard was more relaxed anyway, which meant it was quite easy for Gabrielle to slip away when Arabella set the young, blonde beauties on her brother.

She hurried outside to the gardens, where she'd arranged to meet Fenworth. From there they'd be on the road to Gretna Green where they could be married at once, and then Gabrielle would retire out to the country. Fenworth could do whatever he did, and Gabrielle could have the quiet life she'd become used to. She'd dreamed of glamor and excitement, but London had proved a little too much for her. Happy endings weren't to be found in the city. She'd be happy with her own house, that she could decorate and run as she wished, with occasional visits from her husband. Children sounded nice as well. She didn't have much use for Fenworth himself, but he would need a child or two and she could raise them, give them the love and happy childhood that she'd always wanted but never had.

Maybe their lives would turn out more like Cordelia's that way, and less like Gabrielle's.

Ugh. Sometimes she was so morose than she hated herself. But she couldn't help it right now – this was the ending to whatever small dreams she'd had left. Now she'd just settle for not being miserable and feeling like she was a child standing outside of a candy store that no one would let her in to.

The garden was dark, almost somber, and dimly lit. That certainly didn't help the feeling of impending doom either. She hurried along the pathway, eager to get to the gazebo where she would meet the Viscount and be off.

"Gabrielle!"

She whirled around at the hissing voice calling her name, shocked. How had her stepmother finished fixing her hem so quickly?! She should have been in the retiring room for much longer! Gabrielle was so shocked that she didn't even move. All her careful planning... and now what?

"Cordelia! Go away!"

"What are you doing?" Cordelia demanded as she finally reached Gabrielle, panting from the effort of her exertions to catch up.

Anger flashed through Gabrielle. Anger and envy and resentment... Cordelia already had it all and now she was getting in the way of the very little that Gabrielle was trying to take for herself. "I told you I would accept the first offer of marriage that I was given, and I have."

"It can't be a worthy offer if you have to sneak away to marry the man," Cordelia said, aghast.

"We're eloping, it's romantic," Gabrielle said in a low voice, even though it was neither. She looked around, but she didn't see anyone else running to catch up with them. It was just her and Cordelia, and Cordelia was not enough to stop her. "Now go away."

"Gabrielle, I'm trying to help you. You can't really want to do this."

"Of course I want to, why else would I be out here? I can't spend one more day in that house, I just can't. I don't want to go to balls anymore, I just want to be married and go live in the country, away from... from *everyone*." She knew Cordelia would hear the ring of truth in her words. She was starting to feel almost desperate to get the other woman away. This had to end, tonight, and her plan had worked almost perfectly, up until now. It could still work perfectly. "If you want to help, go distract everyone until I'm gone."

"No. Whatever is wrong, Gabrielle, we can work it out. We'll talk to Philip and-"

"No! Just go away. If you won't distract them, just don't tell them where I've gone or the second your husband catches up to me I'll tell him all about how you trapped him into marriage." Gabrielle knew her voice was becoming hard, cruel, but she couldn't stop herself. She felt just like she had whenever she'd tattled on Cordelia to the Baron – not that Cordelia had ever done much that could upset the Baron, but whenever she had, Gabrielle had used that to her advantage.

Cordelia's jaw dropped. "What?- I never- That's a lie!"

"But it's not, that's what makes it so perfect," Gabrielle said with a bitter laugh. "I overheard you and Marjorie talking about inviting him to the house party, one of a few gentlemen, and how you would be able to entice him into marrying you."

She didn't know if the Marquess would care or not, but he might. If there was even the chance this would make Cordelia go away, Gabrielle was willing to take it. She wasn't bluffing either. If Cordelia wouldn't leave her alone, she was perfectly willing to try and take down the other woman with her. She doubted Cordelia would want to risk it. Cordelia was such a people pleaser, she wouldn't want Philip to know.

But her stepmother took a deep breath and straightened her spine. "Tell him whatever you wish, but I am not letting you do this. If you don't turn around right now and come back to the house with me, I will go straight to Philip and bring him out here. I might not have the strength to drag you back inside, but he certainly does."

Bristling, Gabrielle gaped at her. "You can't do that!"

"I can, and I will."

"But I'll tell him everything! He'll never trust you again! He'll know what a scheming charlatan you are!" Gabrielle's voice got higher, louder, and Cordelia winced. Everything was truly breaking apart. Where had Cordelia dug up the gumption for this?

"I hope he knows me better than that," Cordelia replied in a low voice. "If nothing else, despite what I may or may not have done in the past, I will not betray his trust now. I will not provide you with a distraction or assist you in disrespecting my husband's authority over you as his ward."

"I appreciate that Cordelia." Philip's deep tones struck both of them silent.

No... no, no, no. Agony cracked through Gabrielle. It had all been for naught. She and Cordelia both turned to look.

The Marquess was standing there, his face grimly blank in the moonlight. Directly behind him was Felix, Lord Hyde, and Eleanor, all with grim expressions on their faces. Eleanor was the only one who looked at all sympathetic.

"We need to leave. Now." His voice cracked like a whip, indicative of the emotions he was holding inside.

Gabrielle groaned and sagged, as if she were a puppet whose strings had just been cut. So close... she'd been so close.

THE LOOK of utter defeat on Gabrielle's face made Felix's chest hurt. He couldn't imagine why she would look so, unless... had she arranged to meet a man that she'd fallen in love with? One whom she didn't think Philip would approve of? He couldn't imagine another reason why she would risk doing so again, unless there was true emotion involved.

Rabid jealousy tasted bitter on his tongue. He'd waited too long.

Flanking her, with Philip on the other side, and Lord Hyde bringing up the rear, they turned to follow the path back to the house. Lady Hyde and Cordelia had already gone on ahead, walking much faster. He figured Cordelia was probably rather distressed by her stepdaughters behavior. She'd certainly looked upset.

Not far from the entrance to the gardens, there was a scuffle and a few shouts. Recognizing his brothers' Thomas and Walter's voices, as well as a third he couldn't quite place, the men all glanced at each other and hurried forward. Felix grabbed a hold of Gabrielle's arm, making sure she stayed with them. She looked at him in something like alarm, but kept up. They came into the light to see Cordelia and Eleanor hovering a few steps away from the drama, which was between them and the house.

Standing between Thomas and Walter, hands on his hips as he demanded they let him pass, Viscount Fenworth looked past them to see Philip's party, with Gabrielle at its center.

"There she is!" he shouted loudly, drawing even more attention from the balcony beside the ballroom, where a small crowd was already gathering. He pointed dramatically at Gabrielle, whose cheeks had gone bright red. "I told you my bride was waiting for me!"

Felix muttered a curse. Fenworth? She'd been meeting Fenworth?

He didn't know whether to shake her or grab her and take her away to save her from herself.

Worse, with his announcement, Fenworth had just ruined any chance they had at smoothing over a scandal. Even though Gabrielle had obviously returned from the gardens well chaperoned, between her dance with the man last night, his shouted accusation, and the fact that she'd gone to meet him tonight, assumptions would be made. Gabrielle's reputation was effectively ruined, despite their attempt to save her from her poor choices.

"Waiting for you? I was taking a walk in the garden with my friends, and I'm already married," Eleanor said haughtily, looking at Fenworth like he was a worm. Felix couldn't help but bark a laugh at her audacity, even though he knew the damage was already done.

Fenworth went red in the face, his fists clenching at his sides. "Not you, the Lady Gabrielle of course! My bride-to-be!"

"*We*," Eleanor emphasize the word as she turned back to stand next to Gabrielle on the other side, hooking her arm with Gabrielle's, "were walking in the garden."

"She wasn't with you when you left the ballroom a few minutes ago," Fenworth shot back.

"That's enough, Fenworth," Philip growled, glancing around the growing crowd. Felix knew exactly what his friend was thinking. The best thing they could do was remove themselves from the situation as quickly as possible, regroup, and figure out what to do now. He especially wanted to get Gabrielle away from Fenworth; she didn't look like a woman in love and she was trembling. He softened his grip on her arm, angling himself so that he was standing a bit in front of her, between her and Fenworth.

"I suppose I should come with you," Fenworth said smugly, smirking at Philip. "We'll need to discuss arrangements."

Philip stared him down coldly. "I see no reason to do so."

The look on Fenworth's face was almost comical, despite the seriousness of the situation. The Viscount sputtered. "No one else will have her now! She has to marry me!"

"You-!" Gabrielle's outraged sputter turned into a gasp of shock as Felix suddenly sprung forward, planting his fist firmly in the Viscount's jaw. It was the second time he'd done it for her and he didn't regret it for a moment. Bloody bastard. He had no honor.

Chaos descended as Fenworth went down, Felix on top of him. He could hear Gabrielle shrieking at him to stop, but he drew back his fist for another go until her small hands grabbed his arm. Just in time, he stopped his backward motion, just barely keeping from elbowing her in the face.

Cordelia had grabbed onto Gabrielle, trying to hold her back and Philip was holding onto her... bloody hell, this was turning into a mess. The close call he'd almost had with accidentally hitting Gabrielle turned his blood cold.

"What were you thinking?" Felix bellowed at her, pulling her away from the fallen Viscount. "You could have been hurt jumping in like that!"

"What were *you* thinking?!" she shrieked back at him. "He's a Viscount! You can't just attack him!"

"I'll hab you up on chargesh for dis!" Fenworth's muffled words punctuated her retort as he held his nose, which was bleeding heavily.

Thomas, a future viscount himself, loomed over Fenworth. Ha, as if Felix's family would ever let a worm like Fenworth come after him. "Get the hell out of here while you still can, unless you wanted to face attempted kidnapping charges."

"We were elobing!" The Viscount scrambled away as Felix turned towards him again, still holding his nose.

"Unless you want an appointment at dawn, leave *now.*"

Fenworth paled. Felix had quite a reputation as both a fencer and a crack shot, whereas Fenworth's activities were much less... active. Duels were illegal, although still fought on occasion, and Fenworth would probably hide behind that when pressed. For now, he just whimpered and scampered away into the shadows of the garden. Good riddance.

Turning to Gabrielle, fists clenched at his side, Felix opened his mouth, but he couldn't even think of what words he wanted to say, he was so incensed. Before he managed to come up with any, Philip was grasping Gabrielle by her arm.

"We're leaving. *Now.*"

Felix gritted his teeth, but there was nothing to be done. The titters and whispers of the *ton,* who had received a bird's eye view of the dramatics from the balcony above, followed them. Gabrielle had left her guardian with very few options now. Of course Philip and Cordelia would back her, as would their families, but the damage to her reputation was done.

Unless, of course, some willing gentleman stepped in to save her. This wasn't exactly how Felix had seen his marriage beginning, but it wasn't just Gabrielle's fault. She was a young lady, new to London and its dangers; her guardians were necessarily involved with each other as they were new to their marriage and he… he had let his focus on her lapse. He felt he carried part of the blame. If he hadn't stepped back from Gabrielle following the incident with Mr. Pressen, he would have been much more in tune with her mind. Plus, Lady Winchester would never have had the opportunity to get her hooks in him. Felix had allowed himself to be distracted even though he knew that Gabrielle needed careful handling, not to mention attention, and she wasn't backwards about going looking for it. If he'd played his cards right, perhaps she would have gone looking for attention from him, not a cad like Fenworth.

He could have charmed her if he'd truly wanted to. Seduced her.

Turned her head and made her starry-eyed. Instead he'd prodded and poked her, delighting in her stormy responses, and then abandoned her at a time when she could have used a stalwart companion. Given her the opportunity to turn to someone else, practically pushed her into it in fact by making it clear that she wasn't going to receive the attentions she wanted from him. His own uncharacteristic hesitation and indecision about whether or not to actively court Gabrielle had left her vulnerable to the worst of the fortune hunters.

Gabrielle was ultimately responsible for her own actions, of course, but at the same time, he couldn't help but feel that he'd failed her.

~

"I'M GOING TO MARRY HER."

Philip didn't even raise an eyebrow at Felix's declaration, but he didn't respond either. It was like Felix hadn't even spoken, as Philip went straight to his liquor supplies. Not that Felix was going to argue with that response; after the scene in the gardens with Fenworth and the silent carriage ride back to Dunbury House, he could certainly use a drink. Strangely, the thought of marriage didn't at all factor into that need.

Accepting the glass from Philip's hand, Felix cleared his throat. "I'm going to marry her. It's the only way."

"The only way, what?" Philip asked, his expression deceptively bland, as he settled into one of his armchairs. His fingers stroked over the wide armrest for a moment, while he lifted his glass to his lips with the other hand and took a long swallow.

"The only way to save her reputation."

"And is that the only reason you want to marry her?" Philip asked, never losing the blandness to his features, although his hazel eyes pinned Felix with his gaze.

"No." He would have left it at that, but Philip raised his eyebrow, obviously waiting for a more thorough response. Felix sighed. "I've had it on my mind for a while."

"So you said, but you never acted on it."

"I was still thinking it over."

"And now that she's ruined, and you can play hero, you're ready to swoop in and save the day."

Now Philip was being deliberately antagonistic and Felix scowled at him, his temper rising as he tightened his fingers around the glass he was holding. "No, I'd have preferred she wasn't ruined, but I don't care that she is. I should have been more forward about courting her before but... Look, I want the kind of marriage you and Cordelia have, that Edward and Eleanor, and Hugh and Irene have. I wasn't sure I could have that with Gabrielle, but... I think we could."

"*Think* isn't good enough."

"Fine," Felix snapped out. He didn't mean to let his temper get the best of him, but it had been a trying night; still, he knew that Philip was just looking out for Gabrielle's best interests, and despite stating several times that he was interested, Felix truly hadn't acted upon that interest. "I'm determined to have that kind of marriage and I want it with Gabrielle."

Philip smiled at him, completely calm and unruffled. "That's all I wanted to hear."

"You're bloody impossible sometimes," Felix grumbled, tipping back his glass and drinking the alcohol in one burning slide of liquid. Philip just smiled wider.

"Well, if you couldn't admit it to me, how would you ever admit it to her? I think you're just what Gabrielle needs, but only if you're willing to step up and put forth the effort."

"I am."

"Good, then it's decided. Special license?"

"Yes." Feeling decidedly calmer now that his decision had been made and events were in motion, Felix tapped his finger against his empty glass. "Manchester should be willing to help, he felt a measure of responsibility for tonight's ah, events. I can go straight there from here and have everything arranged for tomorrow."

"Tomorrow?" Philip raised one eyebrow, looking almost surprised.

"Tomorrow," Felix said firmly. The longer they waited, the more time the *ton* would have to gossip about Gabrielle; this way the gossip would be refocused on their sudden marriage. Which, actually, meant that punching Fenworth had done him a favor, even though Fenworth was a Viscount and Felix was only brother to one. It could be spun as passionate jealousy, which would make his and Gabrielle's sudden marriage romantic to many of the gossips, which would help thwart any damage that more vicious tongues might try to do. But only if they married quickly and then showed a united front to the *ton*.

~

"What are they talking about in there?" Gabrielle asked, agitated, even though she knew Cordelia wouldn't know the answer. Her step-mother couldn't - the Marquess hadn't said a word to her or Gabrielle in the carriage. But she couldn't help but wonder aloud, too anxious to keep her thoughts quiet.

Tonight had been an unmitigated disaster, but in some ways, waiting like this was far worse. Would the Marquess order her from the house? Send her away to the country in disgrace? That might not be so bad, since it was close to her original goal even if she'd be alone and bereft of children, but it would also depend on where he sent her and whether or not he supplied any funds to maintain her. She wished that a spanking, or even a more severe punishment to her poor bottom would suffice... how strange that she actually wanted that now, but there was something comforting about being punished when it was deserved and then being forgiven once the discipline was over.

She just couldn't imagine what the Marquess would want to discuss with Fel- Mr. Hood. Maybe they needed to discuss the ramifications of Mr. Hood actually punching a Viscount. Gabrielle squeezed her eyes shut. She'd never forgive herself if her actions resulted in Mr. Hood somehow being hurt, and she couldn't imagine that Fenworth would take very well to being assaulted, even if he had run off tonight. Surprisingly, part of her actually felt relieved that she wasn't going to have to marry him. He'd been her hope of escape, and yet her future with him had still seemed rather bleak. However, she didn't know whether or not her current situation had anything to recommend it over marriage to Fenworth.

Whatever was happening, whatever was going to happen to her, she just wanted to know.

"They've been in there forever," she muttered, twisting her hands in front of her uselessly.

Cordelia glanced at the clock on the mantle. "It's only been fifteen minutes.... Perhaps I should ring for some tea."

How very like Cordelia, Gabrielle thought despairingly. Whenever something went amiss, no matter what time of day it was, Cordelia rang for tea. It was the English thing to do, she supposed.

"I don't want tea," she said, her tone brusque. As if tea would help anything... She supposed it made Cordelia feel better to have something to do, but it didn't help soothe Gabrielle at all. "I want to know what they're talking about in there." She paced some more, clenching and unclenching her fists as she shook her head, her emotions bubbling upside of her like shaken champagne. "What was that nitwit thinking anyway? Attacking a Viscount!"

"I believe he was thinking that the Viscount in question was attacking your reputation."

Gabrielle couldn't believe how calm Cordelia was about the entire thing. While Mr. Hood's brother was a Viscount, he himself had no title... he could be charged and punished for the attack. "My reputation was already ruined. Fenworth just wanted to ensure I would marry him."

"Why do you want to?" Cordelia asked, peering at Gabrielle from her place on the couch. "You were so happy to leave the country, why would you want to go back?" Her hazel eyes were somber and confused. Gabrielle didn't blame her for her confusion... how could Cordelia possibly understand? When she'd wanted a husband, she'd just gone to a house party and gotten one. She could have had one before the Marquess if Gabrielle hadn't run interference. More than that, she'd managed to catch a husband who doted on her, adored her, and was obviously in love with her.

Maybe Gabrielle could make her understand.

Coming to a halt, she turned to face Cordelia. "You love Dunbury."

"Yes." The answer was so swift, so assured, that a stab of jealousy lanced through Gabrielle's heart. No, it wasn't fair that Cordelia received everything while Gabrielle had nothing, but she'd finally come to realize that it wasn't Cordelia's fault her life was blessed.

"If he loved another, would you want to stay where you had to witness it?"

Her stepmother blinked and then shook her head. "Felix doesn't love Lady Winchester, Gabby, I can promise you that."

Gabrielle just looked at her stepmother. She felt tired and decades older than the other woman at that moment. "Sometimes, Cordelia, you are so very blind."

The door to the room opened, making both of them jump. Gabrielle's heart fluttered, anxiety squeezing her tightly and making it impossible for any other emotion to work its way in. The Marquess came in, as imposing as ever, although looking a bit disheveled with his hair mussed and his cravat undone. He was alone, which was a relief.

She darted towards the Marquess, needing to get her apology in immediately. Not to forestall her punishment, which was richly deserved, but because she needed him to know that she truly regretted that her actions might cause him and Cordelia some trouble with Society. "Philip, I'm sorry. I really am, I didn't want to dishonor you or Cordelia, I swear-"

To her shock, the Marquess reached out and took her hands, making a kind of soothing, shushing noise to quiet her. She looked up at her, blinking in shock.

"Don't worry, you didn't dishonor us."

Something in her chest - not anxiety or pain for once - squeezed tightly and then released. She made an involuntary noise of surprise as he pulled her in for a quick, reassuring embrace.

He patted her back. "Everything's taken care of."

How could he be so calm? So reassuring? The guilt welled up inside of her. Whatever discipline he deemed necessary, she was ready and willing to receive it. Obviously he thought he could fix what she'd done, but even if he was correct, she still deserved to be punished.

"Are you going to punish me?" Strangely, her voice sounded almost eager, although it was also full of fear and anxiety. She wasn't eager for it, was she?

"We'll talk in the morning. Go on up to bed, I need to speak with your stepmother," he said. Feeling confused and a bit lost, Gabrielle nodded and allowed him to lead her to the door. Holding it open for her, the Marquess gave her a warning look. "There will be a maid outside your door and there's a footman watching your window. Do not attempt to leave the house."

Nodding again, Gabrielle hurried away. She hated the guilty feeling hanging over her, almost wishing that the Marquess had punished her. Perhaps he was waiting till tomorrow… and she couldn't help but wonder what he'd meant when he'd said that he'd taken care of everything. She still didn't know what that meant. Had he secured her a place in the country to retreat to away from the scandal? Sent Mr. Hood to bribe the Viscount? – that sounded like a disaster in the making, but not completely out of the realm of possibility. After all, money was the reason the Viscount wanted her anyway and the Marquess might have enough to spare. Perhaps he would lessen the amount in her dowry after this.

Numbly, she headed up to bed, desperately needed the comfort and surcease of thought that sleep would provide. Answers and possibly punishment would come soon enough tomorrow.

EPILOGUE

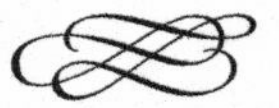

The Archbishop was not thrilled to be roused from his slumber, Duke at his door or no, but he signed the special license all the same. Both Manchester and Felix were effusive in their thanks to the man, and Felix offered up a hefty donation in gratitude. By the time they'd left, the Archbishop had been more amused and interested than irate at having his night of sleep interrupted.

"I'm sorry it's come to this," Manchester said, once they'd returned to the carriage. His brow was furrowed, his lips tilted downward. "Believe me, Arabella is more than sorry for her part in tonight's escapades." He sighed, his lips quirking. "Although, I can't honestly say she would be quite so sorry if it had succeeded. I believe half her disappointment is from knowing they failed. She's very young, in some ways I think this is still all a game to her. Still, it seems a valuable learning experience."

"Don't blame yourself," Felix said. "Gabrielle and Arabella together are a force to be reckoned with. Besides, I can't help but admire their ingenuity."

Manchester snorted. "You wouldn't say that if you had to live with my sister. I am plagued by her ingenuity. Do you know, the chit says she has no interest in being married? She's already turned down three offers from perfectly respectable gentlemen."

"And you allowed her to?" Felix raised his eyebrows at the other man. Even in the darkness of the carriage, he could see Manchester's cheeks color in the passing lamplight. He shrugged his broad shoulders.

"Ah well. I want her to be happy. And an unhappy marriage does not make for a happy life."

All too true, and Felix already knew that he had his work cut out for him, but he was sure that – in the end – he could have that happy life too. Eventually.

FELIX GROANED with relief when he finally returned home to his bachelor's quarters, happy to be done with this day.

Damnation. He grimaced as he realized he was going to have to find new quarters. Immediately. Jermyn Street was no place to bring a respectable woman. Bachelors lived here and only bachelors.

He had several notes to send out, not the least of which would be to his brothers and parents. Felix could only imagine the dramatics his mother would create if she were deprived of being at her son's wedding. She'd be thrilled one of them was finally getting married, and he doubted she would care even if Gabrielle truly had been ruined by Fenworth. Not as long as Felix *wanted* to marry her.

His mother was a true romantic, for which he counted his blessings. There were certainly going to be some who looked at Gabrielle with censure after tonight. A respectable marriage could only do so much. Of course, once the old tabbies realized he was going to be just as faithful to his marriage vows as the much-gossiped about Dunburys, that would calm quite a bit of the talk. The gossips did love a reformed rake, and that Gabrielle would be the one to "tame" him would actually do her quite a bit of good in their eyes.

In the meantime, a hasty marriage and a quick retreat to the countryside where they could cement their bond seemed in order. Felix didn't fool himself into thinking Gabrielle was going to be pleased by his and Philip's solution to her reputation. She'd been like a cat with her fur rubbed the wrong way ever since he'd met her, and - perversely - that had just made him more intrigued by her. If she'd truly wanted to be rid of his attention, she should have fawned on him.

His brother Walter had told him he was sick in the head when Felix had admitted his fascination with Gabrielle and why, and Felix couldn't bring himself to disagree.

Perhaps some of it was the challenge. She had thick walls around her, and he doubted anyone truly knew her. Much of what Cordelia thought of her was pure conjecture based on observation. The same as Felix had been forced to do. None of her suitors seemed to truly see her; they were happy to accept the charming veneer she presented, without trying to see deeper.

Felix wanted to be the one to break through those walls and discover the real Gabrielle. From the small flashes of truth he'd seen, he thought he'd rather like that Gabrielle. The fire inside of her, the brat that never quit – when she wasn't being cruel he liked that side of her – and the loyal friend that she already was to Arabella and Cynthia. Felix hoped that loyalty would be transferred to him as well; he wanted her loyalty, her passion, and even the brat that she could be. He doubted he'd ever be bored.

And it didn't hurt that he'd wanted to bed her from the moment he saw her either. Or that he'd seen the shiver of excitement when he'd bent down and whispered in her ear after Philip and Cordelia's wedding that he'd spank her if she didn't behave herself. Even then, knowing he'd had no right, he hadn't been able to control himself from thinking about it. Fantasizing about it.

Feisty, furious Gabrielle with her flashing green eyes and haughty chin... he'd be all too happy to help with the reformation of her viperish tongue. She'd have been wasted on a man like Pressen or Fenworth. Neither of them could see the true worth of her, the vulnerable waif hiding in her eyes, although he was sure they suspected she was a passionate woman. He doubted either of them would be able to bring those passions to fruition however, because he doubted either of them realized she craved a man to bring her to heel. Philip had told him that the physical discipline he'd instituted had had a very salutary effect on her, and Felix intended to see that didn't go to waste once she was his wife.

Disciplining Gabrielle might take a lifetime, but Felix certainly didn't mind the effort. Not with her.

~

"I WON'T."

"You will."

"I *won't.*" Gabrielle resisted the urge to stomp her foot. Or burst into tears. Or any other number of useless gestures that would get her nothing but a stern look and threat of a red bottom from Lord Dunbury. Her guardian. Her stepmother's husband.

Her stepmother was a lucky woman. Everyone loved her.

And no one loved Gabrielle. Not even the man who was going to marry her.

Tears stung at the backs of her eyes, and she blinked rapidly, her chin going up. "You can't make me."

"I most certainly can," Philip said, his tone going cold. Inwardly she quailed, although she didn't give any visible sign of it. Gabrielle would rather be spanked than have Philip turn off his emotions towards her. She hated it when he looked at her with impatient disgust. She especially hated it when Cordelia would try to intervene.

Life would be so much nicer if she could just hate her stepmother. Did the woman have to be so bloody perfect? Someone should nominate her for sainthood. It was an example Gabrielle could never hope to replicate. Cordelia was patience, sweetness, and light, no matter what happened to her. She saw the best in everyone and every situation. It was like she had sunshine glowing from her very pores. By comparison, Gabrielle felt like a squat toad.

She knew she was beautiful. Men liked her because she was beautiful. But that was an empty kind of admiration. A lonely way to be appreciated. On the inside, she was ugly. Especially in comparison to Cordelia.

"The papers have been signed, Gabrielle. You put yourself into this position, and you should be grateful that Felix was willing to do the honorable thing and put himself forward."

"I'd rather have Fenworth."

Absolute honesty, that. Gabrielle didn't even have to twist the truth. Of course she'd felt a bit relieved when he'd first run off, but if it came to a choice between him and Mr. Hood… Better to be married to a man who wanted her for her money than to a man who would actually tear into her heart day after day after day. The only reason she'd wanted to be married and away from this house was to avoid him.

"Fenworth isn't an option. You'll marry Felix, today." Philip looked at her, and something in his countenance softened. Just a bit. Cordelia must be getting to him too, Gabrielle though bitterly. She was the kind of wife men wanted, the kind they were willing to change for. "He'll take good care of you, Gabrielle."

Of course he would. Because to do anything else would disappoint his darling Cordelia.

Perhaps this was karmic justice, after all her years of being a fairly terrible step-daughter, Gabrielle was going to marry a man who was in love with her stepmother.

It seemed that no matter how she tried to escape it, Gabrielle was destined for a life of unhappiness.

CLICK HERE to read Gabrielle's Discipline and find out what happens next.

ABOUT THE AUTHOR

Golden Angel is a *USA Today* best-selling author and self-described bibliophile with a "kinky" bent who loves to write stories for the characters in her head. If she didn't get them out, she's pretty sure she'd go just a little crazy.

She is happily married, old enough to know better but still too young to care, and a big fan of happily-ever-afters, strong heroes and heroines, and sizzling chemistry.

She believes the world is a better place when there's a little magic in it.

www.goldenangelromance.com

bookbub.com/authors/golden-angel
goodreads.com/goldeniangel
facebook.com/GoldenAngelAuthor
instagram.com/goldeniangel

OTHER TITLES BY GOLDEN ANGEL

HISTORICAL SPANKING ROMANCE

Domestic Discipline Quartet

Birching His Bride

Dealing With Discipline

Punishing His Ward

Claiming His Wife

The Domestic Discipline Quartet Box Set

Bridal Discipline Series

Philip's Rules

Gabrielle's Discipline

Lydia's Penance

Benedict's Commands

Arabella's Taming

Pride and Punishment Box Set

Commands and Consequences Box Set

Deception and Discipline

A Season for Treason

A Season for Scandal

Bridgewater Brides

Their Harlot Bride

Standalone

Marriage Training

CONTEMPORARY BDSM ROMANCE

Venus Rising Series (MFM Romance)

The Venus School

Venus Aspiring

Venus Desiring

Venus Transcendent

Venus Wedding

Venus Rising Box Set

Stronghold Doms Series

The Sassy Submissive

Taming the Tease

Mastering Lexie

Pieces of Stronghold

Breaking the Chain

Bound to the Past

Stripping the Sub

Tempting the Domme

Hardcore Vanilla

Steamy Stocking Stuffers

Entering Stronghold Box Set

Nights at Stronghold Box Set

Stronghold: Closing Time Box Set

Masters of Marquis Series

Bondage Buddies

Master Chef

Dungeons & Doms Series

Dungeon Master

Dungeon Daddy

Dungeon Showdown (Coming 2022)

Poker Loser Trilogy

Forced Bet

Back in the Game

Winning Hand

Poker Loser Trilogy Bundle (3 books in 1!)

SCI-FI ROMANCE

Tsenturion Masters Series with Lee Savino

Alien Captive

Alien Tribute

SHIFTER ROMANCE

Big Bad Bunnies Series

Chasing His Bunny

Chasing His Squirrel

Chasing His Puma

Chasing His Polar Bear

Chasing His Honey Badger

Chasing Her Lion

Night of the Wild Stags

Chasing Tail Box Set

Chasing Tail… Again Box Set

Made in the USA
Monee, IL
19 May 2021